He sounds like he's selling a bill of goods.

Her thoughts ran rampant, wondering what kind of bargain had been struck between her pa and this man. Delphinia was not told the particulars and she knew her pa would never divulge all of the information to her. She knew he just wanted fo be free of any responsibility. Ever since Mama had died, all he could talk about was his going to search for gold and how he would be rich and free of his worries. He had talked about it for years, but Mama had always managed to keep him level-headed and made him realize that going in search of gold was not the way of life for a married man wih a family.

Well, he was "free" now. Mama had died and Delphinia was being shipped off with this stranger to some unknown place out west. Once again, she began to feel the tears well up in her eyes, but she made up her mind that she would not cry in front of her pa again. If he wanted to be rid of her, so be it. She had no choice in the matter.

Suddenly, she felt a hand reach across hers and heard Mr. Wilshire saying, "Here, I'll take that out to the wagon for you. You tell your pa good-bye and then we'll be on our way. I'll be waiting outside."

JUDITH MCCOY MILLER makes her home in Kansas with her family. *Threads of Love* is her first inspirational romance novel.

Threads
of Love

Judith McCoy Miller

Heartsong Presents

Dedicated to Tracie J. Peterson, with love and heartfelt thanks for your friendship, encouragement, and prayers.

A note from the author:
I love to hear from my readers! You may write to me at the following address: **Judith McCoy Miller**
Author Relations
P.O. Box 719
Uhrichsville, OH 44683

ISBN 1-57748-051-1

THREADS OF LOVE

Cover illustration by Kay Salem.

one

The sounds in the kitchen caused Delphinia to startle awake
and she immediately felt the dreadful taste of bile rise in her
throat. Jumping from her bed, she ran to the washstand,
removed the pitcher, and expelled the few remains of last
night's supper into the chipped bowl. Looking into the small
mirror that hung over the washstand, she was met by a
ghostly likeness of herself. *I can't bear this, I just can't,* she
thought as she rinsed her mouth and reached for a small linen
towel to wipe her perspiring forehead. Making her way back
to bed, she wrapped herself in a quilt and prayed that this
was a bad dream.

"Oh please, dear Lord, let me go to sleep and wake up to
my mama's laughter in the kitchen. Let this all be a horrible
nightmare."

Instead, she heard her father's harsh command, "I hear ya
awake in there, Delphinia. This ain't no day to be lazin'
around. You get yourself dressed and do it *now*. You still got
things to pack and time's gettin' short."

"I know, Pa, but I'm feeling poorly. Maybe you'd better
tell that man I won't be able to go with him. I'm sure he
won't want some sickly girl," she replied in a feeble attempt
to dissuade him.

She heard her father's heavy footsteps come across the
kitchen floor toward her room, knowing that she had tested
his patience too far. The bedroom door swung open and he
said in a strained voice, "Either you get yourself dressed or
you'll travel as you are."

"Yes, Pa," she answered, knowing her efforts to deter him

5

had failed and that she would soon be leaving home.

Trying to keep her stomach in check, she donned a green gingham dress and quickly pinned her hair in place. Not giving much care to her appearance, she sat down on the bed and placed her remaining belongings into the old trunk. Her hands trembled as she picked up a frayed shawl, threw it around her shoulders, and lay back on the bed, willing herself to think of happier days.

The noise outside the house brought her back to the present. How long had she been lying there? The streaming rays of sunlight that patterned the room told her that it must be close to noon. Her heart began to pound and immediately she began pressing down the gathers of her skirt in a slow, methodical motion. There was a loud knock at the heavy wooden door, followed by footsteps and the sound of voices. Minutes passed and then she heard her father calling out her name. She picked up her bonnet and sat staring at it, unwilling to accept that the time of departure had arrived. Her father called out again and she could hear the impatience in his voice. Knowing she dared not provoke him further, she compelled herself to rise from the bed and walk to the kitchen.

There, standing before her, was Jonathan Wilshire, the man who had bargained with Pa to take her away from the only home she had ever known. It was a certainty that she would dislike him. She had prayed and prayed about her predicament, but somehow God had not seen fit to eliminate this man from her life. She had begun praying that his horse would break a leg and he would not arrive. But soon she was asking forgiveness for thinking in such an unkind manner. She briefly considered a plea to God that Mr. Wilshire get lost on the journey, but she knew that would not be a Christian prayer, for he had children at home that required his safe return. So, in desperation, she did as her mama had told her many times: "When you don't know for sure what to pray for, just turn it over to the Lord for He knows your heart and will provide the best way." Fervent prayers had been uttered each night outlining the folly of the decision to send her west and requesting the Lord's assistance in finding a remedy. Although she was not sure what was best for her, she knew that leaving for Kansas with Mr. Wilshire would be a mistake. Given the amount of time she had spent in dissertation, she had been positive the Lord would agree and save her from this pending disaster.

Just look at what results that had produced! Here was Jonathan Wilshire, standing in her kitchen and looking fit as a fiddle, ready to take her to some farm in Kansas and turn her into a mama for his children. Where had her mother ever gotten the notion that praying like that would work?

Her heart had slowed down somewhat and she began to feel outrage and frustration begin to take over. She stepped toward her father and had just begun to open her mouth and voice that anger when, sensing her wrath, he said, "Delphinia, this is Jonathan Wilshire, the gentlemen we have discussed."

Once again, her palms began pressing down the gathers in her skirt and, looking directly at her father, she blurted out, "We never *discussed* Mr. Wilshire, Papa. You merely announced you were sending me away with him."

Delphinia could sense the discomfort she was causing for both men. Feeling she must press any advantage that could be gained, she continued with her tirade. "Papa, I've told you over and over that I don't want to leave you. It's been only a few months since Mama died and I don't want to lose you, too. . .and my home, Papa. Must I leave my home?" Tears had begun to roll down her cheeks and onto the pale green bodice of her frock. Her father stared at her in disbelief. She had never, in all of her seventeen years, questioned his decisions. Now, here she was, humiliating him in front of a total stranger. Not knowing if it was caused by anger or embarrassment, she watched as his short, thick neck and unshaven face quickly began to turn from deep tan to purplish red, clear to his receding hairline. Given the choices, she was hoping for embarrassment because her papa was not easy to contend with when angry. But as soon as their eyes met, she knew he was not only angry, but that he had reached the "boilin' stage" as Mama used to call it. Well, so be it. He was sending her away and she was going to tell him how she felt. After all, she had given God a chance to get things in order and He had certainly missed the mark!

"Delphinia," her father roared, "you will fetch the rest of your possessions immediately and place them in Mr. Wilshire's wagon. We've already loaded the other trunks. I'll hear no more of this nonsense. You know you're goin' along with Mr. Wilshire to look after his children. He's ready to pull out. Now mind your tongue, girl, and do as you're told."

Eyes downcast and knowing that her fate was sealed, she quietly murmured, "Of course, Papa. I'll only be a minute."

Walking back to her room, Delphinia allowed herself one last look at the small dwelling that she had called home for all of her seventeen years. She entered her sparsely furnished bedroom for the last time, grabbed the handle on the side of her trunk, and pulled it into the kitchen.

Making her way toward the center of the kitchen, her father once again began with his issuance of instructions. "Now mind your manners, sis. I've told Mr. Wilshire that you know your reading and writing and can teach his youngsters what schooling they need to know."

Turning to the stranger, he continued his diatribe, "She even knows how to work with her numbers and so if there isn't a school nearby, she'll make a fine teacher for you."

He sounds like he's selling a bill of goods, Delphinia

thought. Besides, all of her studies had been through her mama's efforts. Pa had always said it was a waste of time and had chided Ma for spending time on Delphinia's lessons. But her mother had stood firm and said it was important for both girls and boys to know how to read, write, and do their figures. When Pa would become too obstinate about the subject, Ma would smile sweetly and tell him that no child of hers would be raised not knowing how to read God's Word. Then Pa would back down and Delphinia's lessons would continue. Now here he was, using that bit of education to get rid of her.

Her thoughts ran rampant, wondering what kind of bargain had been struck between her pa and this man. Delphinia was not told the particulars and she knew her pa would never divulge all of the information to her. She knew he just wanted to be free of any responsibility. Ever since Mama had died, all he could talk about was his going to search for gold and how he would be rich and free of his worries. He had talked about it for years, but Mama had always managed to keep him level-headed and made him realize that going in search of gold was not the way of life for a married man with a family.

Well, he was "free" now. Mama had died and Delphinia was being shipped off with this stranger to some unknown place out west. Once again, she began to feel the tears well up in her eyes, but she made up her mind that she would not cry in front of her pa again. If he wanted to be rid of her, so be it. She had no choice in the matter.

Suddenly, she felt a hand reach across hers and heard Mr. Wilshire saying, "Here, I'll take that out to the wagon for you. You tell your pa goodbye and we'll be on our way. I'll be waiting outside."

Delphinia glanced up. Her father's anger had diminished and he looked as though he might feel a bit of remorse. "I'm sorry, Pa, I know I shouldn't have talked to you with such disrespect. Mama would be very unhappy with my behavior. But I don't think she'd be very happy with yours, either," she added. When he gave no response, she continued, "Don't you think she'd want us to be together, now that she's gone?"

"I suppose, Delphinia, your mama would think that. You gotta remember, though, your mama knew I was never one to stay in one place too long. I've been living in the same place for nigh onto twenty years now. I kept my bargain with your ma and we never took off for the unknown lands farther west. But now I just have to go. There's nothing left here for me."

His words were like a knife in her heart. Was she really nothing to him? Could he think so little of her that it was more important to go searching for something he would probably never find?

"I've made proper arrangements for you, girl, and I know you'll be well cared for. Mr. Wilshire has a nice homestead in Kansas and needs help. It's a good arrangement for all of us and once I get settled, I'll let you know my whereabouts. It'll all work out for the best." He bent down, put an arm around her, and started leading her toward the door.

"What's to become of our home? Will I never see it again? You can't just go off and leave it." She pulled back and looked up at him. Her large, brown eyes were once again wet with tears.

"Now never you mind; I've taken care of all of that. Mama and I had to borrow against this place when times was bad and I'm just turning it back over to the bank. I got a little cash to get me going and what with. . .well, I've got enough to get set up when I hit the gold fields." Once again, he was moving her toward the door.

"Oh, Pa, I just don't think I can bear it," she murmured, reaching up and throwing her arms about his neck.

"Now, now, girl, come along. It's all gonna be just fine. . . you'll see," he said, drawing her toward the wagon.

With Mr. Wilshire's help, Delphinia made her way up onto the seat of the buckboard and, without looking back, she raised her hand in a small, waving gesture to her pa.

Mr. Wilshire slapped the reins and the horses moved out.

two

A wave of panic began to take over Delphinia. Here she was, on her way to who knew where, with a man she did not even know and her pa thought it was just fine. And to think she had prayed so fervently about this! God must have been extremely busy when she issued her petitions, because she was absolutely sure that this could not be His plan for her life. Anyone could see this was a mistake. After all, she was only seventeen and she could see the folly of this situation. And God was. . .well, nobody knew how old God was but He was certainly well over seventeen. Surely He would get her out of this mess. There must be some rescue in store for her. That was it! God had already planned her deliverance from Jonathan Wilshire!

Feeling somewhat comforted by that thought, Delphinia realized she hadn't even gotten a good look at Mr. Wilshire since his arrival. She didn't want to talk to him just now, but she was curious. Cautiously she glanced over his way, only to be met by two of the bluest eyes she had ever seen, and they were staring directly into hers.

She was so startled that she blurted out the first thing that came to mind. "Why would you need to come all the way to Illinois to find someone to care for your children?"

He did not answer but let out the deepest laugh she had ever heard.

"Just why is that such a funny question?" she countered.

"Well," he slowly answered, "I've not had a line of ladies waiting at my front door whom I'd consider suitable to meet the needs of my homestead."

Delphinia was not quite sure what that meant but she knew she did not want to pursue the matter further, at least for now. "Why are we traveling to Kansas with a wagon train? Wouldn't it be quicker and easier to travel by train?" she queried, not sure which would be worse: an arduous trip by wagon train or arriving in Kansas quickly.

"You're right. It would be faster by train, and that had been my intention. I arrived in Illinois a couple days before I was to fetch you and I was staying in town, planning to secure you shortly before our train would depart for Kansas. But, the day I arrived in Cherryvale, a group of folks from the wagon train were also in town. Their wagon master had become ill and wasn't able to continue his duties. Of course, they need to keep moving or the snows will stop them in the mountains," he explained.

"What does that have to do with us returning by train?" she interrupted, having expected a simple answer.

"They weren't able to find anyone to help them. The hotel owner heard of their plight and related it to me. I believe God puts us in certain places at certain times for a purpose," he continued. "The folks on this wagon train are good people with a need. I can fulfill that need by leading them as far as Kansas. I've talked with the wagon master and he thinks he'll be able to take over by then. . .probably before."

"But what if the wagon master isn't well by the time we reach Kansas? What if he dies?" she asked. "Then what?"

"Well, I don't believe either of those things will happen. But, if they should, I've talked with the folks on the wagon train and explained I can go no farther. They'll either have to winter in Kansas or find someone else to lead them the rest of the way. They're willing to put their trust in God that this will work, and so am I," he responded.

She was trusting in God, also, but not for the same things as Jonathan Wilshire.

"I'll be needing to pick up our supplies," he stated, pulling the horses to a halt in front of the general store, "so if there's anything you think you might be wanting for the journey, better get on down and come in with me."

"Oh, I'll just trust your judgment, Mr. Wilshire, as I've certainly never purchased supplies for a long journey and wouldn't have any idea what you might be needing," she stated rather smugly. He needn't think he was getting someone here in Illinois who was all that suitable, either! Besides, she hadn't fibbed for she didn't have the faintest idea what might be needed on such a journey.

Delphinia watched him jump down from the wagon and she could not help but admire his strength and size. Her pa was not a small man but Mr. Wilshire was quite tall and his shoulders were remarkably broad. She had never seen a man quite so large. Now that she thought about it, he was somewhat intimidating in his size. Why hadn't she noticed that before? she wondered. She was surprised she hadn't been frightened by him but then he had been sitting down in the wagon before she had actually taken notice of him. *Well,* she determined, *I'll not be afraid of anyone and that includes this giant of a man.*

A loud voice roused her from her thoughts. "Phiney, Phiney, are you sleeping up there?" Delphinia looked down in horror at Mr. Wilshire standing beside the wagon.

"You weren't speaking to me, were you, Mr. Wilshire?" she inquired.

"Of course I was," he stated, wondering who else she thought he might be talking to. "I was asking if you'd be wanting to choose some cloth to make a few dresses and britches for the children. They have a good selection here. . . better than the general store back home. Besides, we'll probably not go into Council Grove going back."

She stared at him, dumbfounded. "No, wait. What was it

you were calling me?"

"Well, your name of course. I was trying to get your attention. Seemed like you were off daydreaming."

"I mean, what name did you call me?" she persisted.

"Phiney. I called you Phiney. Why?" he questioned.

"Mr. Wilshire," she said with as much decorum as she could muster, "my name is *Delphinia*. Delphinia Elizabeth Hughes—not Phiney, not Delphie, and not Della. Why would you ever call me such a name?" she asked in disgust.

He looked up at her and grinned. "Seems a mite formal to me. And you just feel free to call me Jonathan if you like. I been meaning to tell you that anyhow. Mister Wilshire. . . well, that's kind of formal, too. Besides, I always think people are addressing my pa when they call me that."

A frown was etched on Delphinia's face as she looked down at him, her brown eyes flashing fire. "Mr. Wilshire, I do not think my name is too formal. My mother took great care in choosing my name and I am very proud of it."

Jonathan's eyes sparkled with humor as he watched her trying to restrain her temper. If he was any judge, she would soon be stomping her foot to make a point of this whole issue. He knew he should let it drop, but for some reason he was enjoying the display of emotion she was exhibiting for him.

"I'm mighty pleased you're proud of your name, Phiney. I've always thought it was nice if folks liked their names," he said with a benevolent grin. With that, he moved on toward the general store, while calling over his shoulder, "Better hop on down if we're gonna get some yard goods picked out."

It took all her forbearance not to scream after him, "Don't call me Phiney," but before she could give it further thought, he had disappeared into the store.

She was fairly bristling as she climbed down from the wagon, her bonnet askew and with tendrils of blond hair poking out in every direction. Jonathan stood behind some shelves of dry goods and, with wry amusement, watched her dramatic entry with wry amusement. He did not wish to continue upsetting her, but she really was quite a picture to behold, her cheeks turned rosy and skirt gathered up in her fists. Realizing she was looking for him, he stepped out from behind the shelves.

"Glad you decided to come in and have a look around," he grinned. Ignoring his barb, she made her way to the table of yard goods.

"You realize, of course, Mr. Wilshire, that I have no idea what anyone in your home may need. I don't even know who lives there," she proclaimed, wanting to be sure he realized she was not a willing participant in the future that her father had planned.

"Guess you've got a point," he commented, leaning against the table and causing it to almost topple with his weight. "There's surely no time for going into that now, so just pick some material you like for boys and girls and maybe some for new curtains. Oh, and Granny might like something for a new dress, too."

Her mouth had formed a large oval by the time he had finished his remarks, but before she could even exclaim, he added, "And don't forget to get something for yourself, too."

Not waiting for a reply, he immediately moved on to look at tools and Delphinia found herself staring back at the clerk, an older woman she had never seen before, who was impatiently waiting to take Delphinia's order and get to other customers. Having never before had such a task placed before her, Delphinia smiled pleasantly and approached the expectant clerk. "I'll take some of each of these," she said, pointing to six different fabrics.

Delphinia straightened her shoulders, her arms crossed in front of her and stood there, waiting. When the clerk made no move to cut the yard goods, Delphinia, looking perplexed, urged her on, stating, "That's all I'll be needing. You can cut it now."

"Would you care to give me some idea just how much you'd like of each fabric?" the clerk questioned in a hushed voice and added a smile.

Sensing that she had the sympathy of this woman, Delphinia answered, "Just whatever you think I should have."

"I'll cut enough for curtains to cover four windows out of this cream color, and you'll be able to get a dress for your little girl and a skirt for you out of this blue calico. Let's see, we'll cut a measure of this heavy fabric for some britches for your little boys and this brown print might make up into a nice dress for your grandmother."

Delphinia watched in absolute astonishment. Did this woman actually think she looked old enough to have a husband and houseful of children? Well, she was not about to explain her circumstances to a total stranger. She would just smile and take whatever help the Lord provided and He certainly knew she needed all the help she could get. Of course, *Mr.* Wilshire was also going to need all the help he could get for she was going to educate him to the fact that he had chosen the wrong person for his Kansas family.

"Will you be wanting any thread or lace to go along with this?"

Delphinia was so deep in thought that the question caused her to startle to attention. "Whatever you think. I'll just trust your judgment," she smiled.

The clerk finished quickly, wrapped the goods in brown paper, and tied it with heavy twine. Jonathan moved forward and requested the clerk to add the cost to his other purchases, which were being totaled, and he began to usher Delphinia out of the store.

Turning back, Delphinia walked to the clerk and whispered, "Thank you for your help. I'll be praying for you this evening and thanking the Lord for your help."

"Oh, my dear, thank you," the clerk replied. "It was a pleasure to assist you. It's a long trip you're making, but you're young and strong. With that able-bodied husband of yours, you'll do just fine."

"He's not my husband," Delphinia retorted before thinking.

"Oh. Well, I'll certainly be praying for you, too, my dear," the clerk replied.

Delphinia felt her cheeks turn a crimson red and she began to stutter a reply but the clerk had already turned and was helping another customer. Feeling totally humiliated, she briskly made her way out of the store and back to the wagon where Jonathan was waiting.

Without a glance in his direction, she made her way around the wagon and quickly climbed up onto the seat. Not knowing how many people had overheard their conversation, Delphinia was anxious to join the wagon train as soon as possible.

"I thought maybe you'd like to have dinner in town. There's a good restaurant down the street," Jonathan offered.

"I'm not hungry. Let's get going," she answered, her voice sounding somewhat shrill.

"What's wrong?" he questioned.

"Nothing. Let's just go," she replied.

"I'm not going anywhere until you tell me what's wrong," Jonathan said.

Delphinia knew from the set of his jaw that she was not going to have her way. Grudgingly she recounted the conversation, trying to keep as much composure as possible.

"Is that all?" he questioned. "I'll be right back after I explain our situation to the woman," and he started to make his way into the store.

"No, please," she countered. "I'd rather go no further with

this. Let's just go. I'm honestly not hungry."

Sensing her discomfort and not wishing to cause her further embarrassment, Jonathan jumped up onto the seat, flicked the reins, and yelled, "Giddyup," to the team of brown mares.

Neither of them said anything but, as they grew closer to the wagon train camp, Jonathan sensed an uneasiness come over Delphinia. She was moving restlessly on the wooden seat and her hands began pressing the gathers in her skirt, as he had seen her do on several earlier occasions.

In an attempt to make her feel more comfortable, he said, "You'll not be staying in my wagon at night. Mrs. Clauson has agreed you can stay with her." Delphinia did not respond, but he noticed she was not fidgeting quite so much. This pleased him, though he was not sure why.

Slowing the team, he maneuvered the buckboard beside one of the covered wagons that had formed a circle for the night.

"Thought maybe you wasn't gonna make it back afore supper," a voice called out.

"I'd have gotten word to you if we weren't coming back this evening," Jonathan replied as he jumped down from the wagon and held his arms up to assist Delphinia.

As she was making her descent from the wagon, Jonathan matter-of-factly said, "Mr. and Mrs. Clauson, I'd like you to meet Phiney. . .Phiney Hughes. It was *Hughes,* wasn't it?"

He watched her eyes once again take on that fiery look as she very formally stated, "Mr. and Mrs. Clauson, my name is Delphinia Elizabeth Hughes. Mr. Wilshire seems to find it a difficult name. I, however, prefer to be called *Delphinia. . .* not Phiney." Smiling sweetly at the Clausons, she added, "Pleased to meet you both."

Turning, she gave Jonathan a look meant to put him in his place. He grinned back at her, but soon found himself trying to control a fit of laughter when Mr. Clauson replied, "We're real pleased to meet you, too, Phiney."

Not wanting to give him further cause for laughter and certain that a woman would better understand the proper use of her name, Delphinia decided she would discuss the matter of her name privately with Mrs. Clauson.

Jonathan and Mr. Clauson began unloading the wagon and the older woman, while placing her arm around Delphinia's shoulder, said, "Come on over here with me, Phiney. I'm just finishing up supper and we can visit while the menfolk finish unloading."

So much for another woman's understanding, Delphinia decided, moving over toward the fire. Perhaps she should just let the issue of her name drop with the Clausons. After all, once they arrived in Kansas, she would probably never see them again. Mr. Wilshire, though, was another matter!

"Is there anything I can do to help?" Delphinia inquired.

"No, no. Just set a spell and tell me about yourself. You sure are a pretty thing, with all that blond hair and those big brown eyes. Jonathan figured you probably weren't a looker since your pa was willin' to let you go west with a stranger. Thought maybe you couldn't get a husband."

Noting the look of dismay that came over Delphinia's face and the effect her words had on the young woman, Mrs. Clauson hurried to add, "He didn't mean nothin' bad by that. It's just that most folks wouldn't let their daughter take off with a complete stranger, let alone be advertisin' in a paper to. . . Oh, I'm just jumblin' this all up and hurtin' you more. Mr. Clauson says I need to think 'fore I open my mouth. I'm real sorry if I upset you, Phiney."

Lifting her rounded chin a little higher, Delphinia straightened her back and said, "There's no need for you to feel concern over what you've said. After all, I'm sure you've spoken the truth of the matter."

three

Neither Delphinia nor Mrs. Clauson spoke for a time, each lost in her own thoughts. Delphinia was not sure how long she had been reflecting on the older woman's words when she noticed that Mrs. Clauson was about to serve the evening meal.

"It looks like you've about got dinner ready. Shall I ladle up the stew?"

Mrs. Clauson turned toward the large pot hanging over a slow-burning fire and shook her head. "No, no. I'll do it. You just tell the menfolk we're ready. They should be about done unloading the buckboard and can finish up after supper."

Delphinia rose and, after locating the men and announcing dinner, slowly continued walking toward Jonathan's wagon. Jonathan pulled off his wide-brim hat, wiped his brow with a large, dark blue kerchief, and watched Delphinia as she continued toward his wagon. Her head lowered, her shoulders slumped, she was a picture of total dejection.

"Where are you going? You just told us dinner was ready."

Acting as though she did not hear, Delphinia continued along the outer edge of the circled wagons.

"Hey, wait a minute," Jonathan called as he quickened his step to catch up. When he came even with her, she glanced over and said, "I'm not hungry. You go on and eat. Mrs. Clauson's waiting on you."

Realizing something was amiss, Jonathan gently took hold of her shoulders and turned her to face him. "Phiney, you've got to eat. I know it's hard for you to leave your home, but please come have some dinner."

When there was no reaction to his use of "Phiney," he knew she was upset, but she turned and walked back to the campfire with him. She took the steaming plate of food offered by Mrs. Clauson who, Jonathan noted, seemed somewhat downcast.

Giving him a tentative smile, Mrs. Clauson asked, "Would you be so good as to lead us in prayer before we begin our meal, Jonathan?"

Bowing their heads, Jonathan gave thanks for the food provided and asked God's protection over all the folks in the wagon train as they began their journey. Delphinia was surprised, however, when Jonathan proceeded to ask the Lord to give her strength as she left her father and all those she knew to make a new home in Kansas. She was pleased that he cared enough about her feelings to ask God to give her strength. As she looked up at Jonathan after he had pronounced "Amen," he was smiling at her and remarked, "Well, eat up, Phiney." At that moment, she was not sure if she needed more strength to endure leaving home or to put up with his determination to call her Phiney!

As soon as the meal was over, Delphinia and Mrs. Clauson proceeded to wash the dishes while the men finished loading the covered wagon and Jonathan returned the buckboard to town. By the time he got back to the campsite, folks were beginning to bed down for the night.

"Why don't you get the things you'll be needin' for tonight and bring them over to our wagon. We best turn in soon," Mrs. Clauson advised.

Nodding in agreement, Delphinia made her way to the wagon. Climbing in, she spotted the old brown trunk and slowly lifted the heavy lid. Pulling out her nightgown, she caught sight of her beloved quilt. Reaching in, she pulled it out of the trunk and hugged it close.

She was so caught up in her thoughts that Mrs. Clauson's,

"Do you need help, Phiney?" caused her to almost jump out of her skin.

"No, I'm coming," she replied, wrapping the quilt around her and closing the trunk. She made her way down, careful not to trip over the covering that surrounded her.

After preparing for the night, Delphinia and Mrs. Clauson made themselves as comfortable as possible on pallets in the wagon. "Jonathan's been having some Bible readin' for us since he came to our rescue, but since he was gone so late tonight, he said we'll double up on our readin' tomorrow night. The mister and me, well, we don't know how to read much, so it surely has been a pleasure to have Jonathan read the Scriptures for us," she whispered almost ashamedly.

"Oh, Mrs. Clauson, I would have read for you tonight, if I had known," Delphinia replied.

"Why aren't you just the one. Such a pretty girl and bright, too. That Jonathan surely did luck out," she exclaimed.

Delphinia could feel her cheeks grow hot at the remark and knew it was meant as a compliment. All the same, she wished Mrs. Clauson would quit making it sound like Jonathan had just secured himself a wife.

Bidding the older woman good night, Delphinia spent a great deal of her prayer time petitioning the Lord to execute His rescue plan for her as soon as possible. She did give thanks for the fact that Jonathan seemed a decent sort and that she would have Mrs. Clauson with her for the journey. Once she had finished her prayers, she reached down and pulled the quilt around her, not that she needed the warmth for, in fact, it was nearly summer. Instead, it was the security that the wonderful quilt gave her, almost like a cocoon surrounding her with her mama's presence and love.

Many hours of love and laughter had been shared in completing what had seemed to Delphinia an immense project. Now, she was somewhat in awe that her mother had given so much time and effort to teaching her how to sew those many blocks and make the tiny, intricate stitches required for the beautiful pattern she had chosen.

When Delphinia had announced she wanted to make a quilt, her mother had explained it would take many hours of tedious work. She was doggedly determined about the idea, however, and her mother had patiently shown her each step of the way, allowing Delphinia to make and repair her own mistakes on the beloved project. How they had laughed over some of those mistakes and oh, the hours spent ripping out and restitching until it was just right. Mama had always said that anything worth doing was worth doing right. And when that last stitch had been sewn and the quilt was finally completed, Mama had abundantly praised her hard work and perseverance. She had even called for a celebration and, using the good teapot and china plates, served Delphinia some of her special mint tea and thick slices of homemade bread, smeared with strawberry preserves.

Tears began to slide down Delphinia's cheeks as she thought of those wonderful memories. Had it been only three years since she had enjoyed that special celebration? It seemed an eternity. In fact, it seemed like Mama had been gone forever, yet she knew it wasn't even six months since she had died. Sometimes she had trouble remembering just what her mother looked like and yet other times it seemed that Mama would walk in the door any minute and call her for supper or ask for help hanging a curtain. How she missed her and the stability she had brought to their home! It seemed to Delphinia that her life had been in constant change and turmoil since the day Mama died.

Delphinia closed her eyes, hoping that sleep would soon overtake her. Her mind wandered back to stories her mother had related of how she had come west to Illinois after she and Pa had married. Mama had tried to convince him it

would be a better life for them back east but he was bound
and determined to see new lands. It had been a difficult trip
for Mama. She had lived a life of relative ease. Having been
born the only daughter in a family of six boys had been cause
for much jubilation and, when she later contracted rheumatic
fever as a child, it had made her family all the more determined to protect her. Delphinia remembered Mama talking
about all those uncles and the grandparents she had never
known. Mama had made certain that Delphinia knew that her
grandfather had been a preacher and that he had held great
stock in everyone's learning how to read—not just the boys.
He had made sure that Delphinia's mama was taught the
same lessons as the boys. In fact, she had gone to school
longer than any of the boys so that she could receive a teaching certificate, just in case she did not get married. Her pa
wanted to be sure she would have a respectable profession.
But she did get married. She told Delphinia about meeting
Papa at a tent revival meeting the family had attended in a
nearby town. They started to keep company shortly after that
and were married six months later. Less than two months
after the ceremony, they made their trip west to Illinois.

They had settled in a small house a few miles from
Cherryvale. Pa had gone to work for the blacksmith who
owned the livery stable. Delphinia knew her mama had been
lonely. They did not get to town often and she had longed for
the company of other people. Papa would give in and take
them to church about once a month to keep Mama in better
spirits, but he was usually anxious to get home afterward.
Mama always loved it when there would be a picnic dinner
after services in the summer and everyone would gather
under the big elms, spread out their lunch, and visit or when
the preacher would hold Bible study in the afternoon. Papa
had always seemed uncomfortable and would stay to himself
while Mama fluttered from person to person, savoring each

moment. Papa was not much of a church goer and had never studied the Bible. His folks had not seen any reason for his learning to read or write. They felt children were needed to help with the chores and plow the fields. Delphinia remembered Mama telling her how much she had wanted to teach Papa to read but he had put her off saying he was too old to learn. Sometimes, when Mama would be teaching Delphinia, Papa would become almost angry and storm out of the house. Mama always said it was nothing to worry about, that Papa just needed a breath of fresh air. Maybe, Delphinia thought, Papa was angry at himself because he hadn't let Mama teach him and now his little girl knew how to read and he didn't. Strange she hadn't thought of that before tonight.

She reflected on the time shortly before Mama's death, when she had overheard their hushed talk about not having money. That must have been when Papa borrowed against the house and how they had managed to make ends meet until Mama died. When she once questioned about money, her mother had told her there was time enough for that worry when you became an adult and that she should not concern herself. Her parents had never included her in any family business or, for that matter, anything of an unpleasant nature. She had always been protected. . .until now.

Burrowing farther under the quilt, Mrs. Clauson's remark about Pa advertising to send her west was the last thought that lingered in her mind as she drifted into a restless sleep.

four

Delphinia bounced along on the hard wooden seat, the blistering sun causing rivulets of perspiration to trickle down the sides of her face. She could feel her hair turning damp under the bonnet she was forced to wear in order to keep the sun from scorching her face. It seemed she had been traveling forever and yet, in spite of the heat and dust, she found joy in the beauty of the wildflowers and rolling plains.

Except for the short period of training that Jonathan had given her on how to handle the wagon and team, or those times when it was necessary to cross high waters and climb steep terrain, Jonathan rode his chestnut mare and few words passed between them. She was somewhat surprised when today he had tied his horse to the back of the wagon and climbed up beside her. Taking the reins from her hands, he urged the team into motion and, with a slight jolt, they moved forward in the slow procession taking them farther west.

"Sorry we haven't had more opportunity to talk," Jonathan commented, "but it seems I'm needed more to help keep the train moving. Besides, you've been doing just fine on your own with the wagon."

Delphinia did not respond but smiled inwardly at his compliment. When Jonathan had told her she would be driving the team, she had nearly fainted dead away. She, who had never handled so much as her pa's mules, was now expected to maneuver a team of horses and a lumbering wagon. With Jonathan's patience and her determination, she had finally mastered it, at least well enough not to run into the wagon in front of her.

"We're getting close to home and I thought we should talk a little beforehand about what you can expect," Jonathan stated.

Delphinia expelled a sigh of relief. Finally, he was going to acquaint her with what lay ahead. Nodding her encouragement that he continue, she gave a slight smile, folded her hands and placed them on her lap.

"My brother, Jacob, and his wife, Sarah, died some four months ago. Since that time Granny, that would be Sarah's mother, has been staying in the big cabin with the children. She's become quite frail and isn't able to handle five children and do chores any longer. Tessie, she's the oldest, doesn't think she needs anyone else to help out. At twelve, she's sure she can raise the others and take care of everything on her own."

Delphinia's face registered confusion and alarm. "Are you telling me the children I'm to take care of aren't yours? They are your brother's children? That there are five of them under age twelve? And I will be caring for all of them as well as doing chores and nursing their ill grandmother?" she questioned in rapid succession.

"Whoa, wait a minute," he laughed. "How can I answer your questions if you throw so many my way I can't even keep them straight?"

"I'm glad you find this a matter to laugh about," she exclaimed, feeling tears close at hand and not wanting to cry, "but I'm not at all amused."

"I'm really sorry, Phiney. I guess because I know the situation, it doesn't seem all that bleak to me. You'll get used to it, too. It's just a matter of adjustment and leaning on the Lord. The children are fine youngsters and although the older ones are having a little trouble dealing with the deaths of their folks, they're a big help."

"Just what ages are the children?" she asked, almost afraid to hear the answer.

"Well, there's Tessie, she's twelve and the oldest. She has the prettiest mop of red ringlets hanging down her back, which, I might add, match her temper. She also has a bunch of freckles, which she detests, right across the bridge of her nose. She's not very happy that I'm bringing you home to help out. She thinks she's able to cope with the situation on her own even though she knows her ma and pa wouldn't want it that way. They'd want her to have time to be a little girl and get more schooling before she starts raising a family and taking care of a household. She's had the most trouble dealing with the deaths of her parents. Then there's Joshua; we call him Josh. He's seven and all boy. A good helper, though, and minds real well. He misses his ma's cooking and cheerfulness. I've tried to fill some of the gaps left by his pa. Then there's Joseph. We call him Joey, and he just turned four. He follows Josh around and mimics everything his big brother does, or at least gives it a good try. He doesn't understand death, but we've told him his folks are with Jesus and he'll see them again when he gets to heaven. I think he misses his ma most at bedtime. Then there are the twins, Nathan and Nettie. They're eight months old now and quite a handful. I guess that just about sums up the situation," he said, giving the horses a slap of the reins to move them up closer in line.

"Sums it up?" Delphinia retorted. "That doesn't even begin to *sum it up.*"

"Well," he drawled, "why don't you just ask me questions and I'll try to answer them. . .but one at a time, *please.*"

"All right, number one," she began, with teeth clenched and eyes fixed straight ahead, "why did you tell my pa you needed someone to help with *your* children if they're your brother's children?"

"From the way you asked that question, Phiney, I'm sure you think I concocted a whole string of untruths, presented them to your pa, and he just swallowed it like a fish swallowing bait. Believe me, that's not the way it was. He knew the truth. He knew the children weren't mine. I wrote him a letter telling him of my need and explaining the urgency for a young woman to help out."

"My pa can't read," she interrupted, sure she had caught him in a lie.

Leaning forward and resting his arms across his thighs in order to gain a look at her, he answered, "I know, Phiney. He had a friend of his, a Mr. Potter, read the letter to him and write to me. Mr. Potter started out the letter by telling me your pa could neither read nor write but he was corresponding on his behalf."

Delphinia knew what Jonathan said was probably the truth. After Ma had died when there was anything he did not want her to know about, Pa would get Mr. Potter at the bank to help him.

Jonathan watched as Delphinia seemed to sift through what he had said. It was obvious her father had told her very little about the plan he had devised, or the correspondence and agreement that had followed. Not one to keep secrets, Jonathan asked, "Is there anything else you want to know?"

"Yes," she responded quietly. "Did you pay my pa for me?"

"No. That wasn't the way of it. You're not a slave or some kind of bonded person. I don't own you."

"But you did give him money, didn't you?" she questioned.

"Well—"

"Did you or didn't you give my pa money, Mr. Wilshire?" she determinedly inquired.

"There was money that exchanged hands, but not like I

was buying you. He needed some financial help to get started with his prospecting and said he'd pay it back when he had a strike. I told him it wasn't necessary. I guess if you had to liken it to something, it was more like a dowry. . .only in reverse." Noting the shock that registered on her face at that remark, he continued, "Course we're not gettin' married so maybe that's not a good way to explain."

Delphinia could feel herself shrinking down, total humiliation taking over her whole being. How could her pa have done this to her? How could he think so little of her he would sell her to a total stranger? She was his flesh and blood. . .his only child. She had never felt so unloved and unwanted in her life.

She did not know how far they had come when she finally said, "Mr. Wilshire, please, would you explain how all of this happened to me?"

The question confirmed his earlier belief that her father had intentionally kept her uninformed. Her voice was so soft and sad he couldn't possibly deny the request.

"I'll tell you what I know. Please understand, I won't be speaking for your pa or why he made his decisions. Only the choices I made. . .and the reasons."

When she did not respond but merely nodded her head, he continued. "Well, now, I've told you about the deaths of my brother and his wife. I had come out to Kansas a year or so after them because Jake thought if I homesteaded the acreage next to his, we could work the land together. You know, help each other. I wanted to move west and he thought it would give us an advantage. Sarah and Jake built their house near the western boundary of their land so when I arrived, we constructed a cabin on the eastern boundary of my tract, allowing me to be nearby. We'd always been close and we decided it would be good for both of us. And we were right. It has been good for all of us. . .or at least it was until now. Jake and Sarah brought Granny Dowd with them when they came west. Sarah's pa was dead and she didn't want to leave her mother alone. Granny's been a real wonder to all of us. What a worker! She was just like a little whirlwind, even when I came out here. Then about a year ago, she took ill and just hasn't snapped back to her old self. She seems to rally for a while, but then she has to take to her bed again. She was always a big help to Sarah. I'm sure you'll like her, Phiney. She loves the Lord, her grandchildren, and the West, in that order." He smiled and glanced over at the dejected looking figure jostling along beside him, hoping for some sort of response.

Finally, realizing he was not going to continue further, Delphinia looked over and was greeted by a slight smile and his blue eyes, full of sympathy. "You needn't look at me like you're full of pity for me or my situation, Mr. Wilshire. After all, you're the cause of this," she criticized.

"I didn't cause this, Miss Hughes," he replied. "I merely responded to your pa's ad in the newspaper." *Why can't this woman understand it was her father who was at fault?*

"Ah, yes, the newspaper advertisement. I'd like to hear about that," she retorted, her face flushed not only from the rising sun, but the subject under discussion.

"Well," he fairly drawled, "it appears we're getting ready to stop for the noon meal. I think we better finish this discussion after dinner when you're not quite so hot under the collar. Besides, I don't plan on discussin' this in front of the Clausons," he said as he pulled the team to a stop and jumped down.

He watched in absolute astonishment as she pushed away the arms he extended to assist her, lost her footing, and almost turned a complete somersault at his feet.

Looking up at him, her bonnet all cockeyed and her skirt clear to her knees, she defiantly stated, "I meant to do that."

"I'm sure you did, Phiney. I'm sure you did," he laughed as he began to walk toward the rear of the wagon to untie his mare.

"You could at least help me up," she hollered after him.

Glancing over his shoulder, he grinned and remarked, "Why would you need my help? I thought you planned that whole performance!" She could hear him chuckling as he led his horse down to the small creek.

"Oooh, that man," she mused, as she gathered herself up and proceeded to brush the dust from her dress and straighten her bonnet. "The Lord has a lot of work to do with him yet!"

≈

Delphinia and Mrs. Clauson had just finished preparing the noon meal when Jonathan strode up to the older woman. "Phiney's wanting to be alone and talk to me, Mrs. Clauson, so I thought we'd take our plates down by the creek and eat, if you don't mind. I understand we're going to be makin' camp here since the Johnsons have a wagon wheel that needs repairing before we continue. It's been agreed that this is a fine spot to spend the night. Besides, we've traveled a considerable ways and the rest will do us all good."

"I don't mind at all. You two go on and have a chat. I can sure understand you wanting some time alone," she said with a knowing grin.

Delphinia was positively glaring at him as he said, "Come along, Phiney. Let's go down by the water." He smiled, noting her feet appeared to have become rooted to the spot where she was standing. "I thought you wanted some answers, Phiney. Better come along. I may not have time later."

She did not want to give in and let him have his way. It was childish of her to act peevish over such a little thing. Her mother had always told her to save her arguments for the important issues. Perhaps this was one of those times she should heed that advice. Besides, if she did not go, he might hold true to his word and not discuss the matter later. Picking up her plate and cup, she followed along, calling over her shoulder, "We'll not be long, Mrs. Clauson," only to hear Jonathan respond, "Yes, we will." Mrs. Clauson merely smiled and nodded.

Hurrying to catch up, Delphinia watched as her coffee sloshed out of the metal cup, dribbling onto her apron. "Don't walk so fast. Your legs are longer than mine and I can't keep up," she chided, angry that he once again had the last word.

"I'm sure that haughty little temper of yours gives you enough strength to keep up with anyone," he retorted.

"You needn't make unkind remarks, Mr. Wilshire," she exclaimed.

"I needn't make unkind remarks?" he exploded. "I've been listening to your thoughtless insinuations and comments all morning, but when I point out that you've got quite a little temper, you call that an unkind remark. I'd find that funny if I weren't so aggravated with you right now." He plopped himself down in the shade of a large tree that overhung the stream of water, and shoved a large forkful of beans into his mouth.

"You have control over my life, but don't expect me to be happy about it. I'm not one to apologize unless I feel it's in order, Mr. Wilshire. However, since I don't know all that occurred between you and my pa, I will, just this once, offer my apology. Of course, I may withdraw it after I've heard all you have to say about this odious matter," she informed him authoritatively.

"Odious? Well, that's extremely considerate of you, *Miss Hughes*," he responded, trying to keep the sarcasm from his voice but missing the mark.

Settling on the grass not far from him, she arranged her skirt and commanded, "You may now continue with your account of what occurred between you and my father, Jonathan."

He was so startled she had called him Jonathan, that he didn't even mind the fact that he had been given a direct order to speak. "I believe we left off when you asked about the newspaper advertisement," he began.

She nodded in agreement and he noticed she was again pressing the pleats in her skirt with the palm of her hand as he had observed on several other occasions. *Must be a nervous habit,* he decided to himself.

"I've been trying to find help ever since Sarah and Jake died, but the few unmarried young women around our area were either, shall we say, unwholesome or looking for a husband in the bargain. Granny Dowd wouldn't accept unwholesome and I wouldn't accept a wife. . .not that I plan to stay a bachelor forever. I want to, you know, marry. . . ," he stammered. "It's just that I plan on being in love with the woman I marry, and sharing the same beliefs and goals. I don't want it to be some sort of bargain—"

"Mr. Wilshire, I really am not interested in your marriage plans. I'm just trying to find out why I'm here," Delphinia interrupted.

"That's what I'm trying to explain, if you'll just quit breaking in! Now, like I said, we didn't seem to find anyone that was suitable. Granny and I kept praying we would find an answer. A few weeks later, I was in town to pick up supplies. While I was waiting for my order to be filled, I picked up an old St. Louis newspaper that someone had left in the store. I looked through the advertisements and noticed one that stated, 'Looking for good home and possible teaching position immediately for my daughter.' There were instructions to write a Mr. Potter at the Union National Bank in Cherryvale, Illinois. I was sure it was an answer to prayer and so was Granny.

"That night, we composed a letter to your pa telling him about Jake and Sarah, the children, and Granny's failing health. We told him we were Christians who tried to live by God's Word and would do everything possible to give you a good home in return for your help with the children and the house. We also told him we would pay you a small stipend each month so you'd have some independence."

Jonathan got up and moved toward the creek. Rinsing off his plate, he continued, "We sent that letter off the very next day and waited anxiously for a reply. When it finally came, we were almost afraid to open it for fear it would be a rejection of our offer. Instead, it started out with Mr. Potter telling us your pa could neither read nor write, and that he was acting as his intermediary. Mr. Potter said your pa was pleased with the idea of your coming out to Kansas, and that I should make arrangements to come to Illinois because he wanted to meet with me personally."

"If that's supposed to impress me as loving, fatherly concern for my well-being, I'm afraid it doesn't persuade me," Delphinia remarked.

"I'm not trying to justify anything. I'm just telling you how it all happened."

"I know. I'm sorry. Please continue and I'll try to keep quiet," she murmured.

"I left Kansas the next morning. When I arrived in town, I went straight to the bank and met with Mr. Potter. He sent for your pa and we met the afternoon I arrived in Cherryvale. I presented him with letters I had secured from our minister and some folks in the community during the time we waited for your father's response. Granny said she was sure you were the Lord's answer, and we were going to be prepared."

Delphinia couldn't help but smile at that remark. It sounded just like something her ma would have said.

"Mr. Potter looked over the letters I had with me, read

them to your pa, and he seemed satisfied that we were upstanding folks who would do right by you. He said he was wanting to go farther west in hopes of striking gold and that it would be no life for a young woman. I agreed with him. . . not just because we needed you, but because I felt what he said was true."

Jonathan paused, took a deep breath, and continued, "He told me he had fallen on hard times and mortgaged his house for just about all it was worth. Mr. Potter confirmed the bank held notes on the property and that your pa was going to deed it back over to the bank for a very small sum of money. Your father said he needed extra funds to get supplies and have enough to keep him going until he hit gold. I gave him some money to cover those expenses, but nobody considered it to be like I was buying you, Phiney. I was just so thankful we had found you, I didn't want anything like your pa needin' a little money to stand in the way. Then when the wagon train needed help, I was sure God's hand was at work in all that was happening."

"Did you ever stop to think that if you hadn't given him the money, I could still be at home, where I belong?" she countered.

"Phiney, your pa had made up his mind he was going to go west and search for gold. Nothing was going to stop him. He'd have taken you with him if he had to, I suppose, but he was right. . .it would have been a terrible life for you. But if you're determined this is not what you want, I'll not fight you. The next town we get close to, I'll put you on a train and send you back to Cherryvale."

"To what?" she asked. "My father's gone and if he isn't, he won't want to see me back. The bank owns our land. I have no one to go to," she said dejectedly.

"Your pa loves you, Phiney. He just has a restlessness that needs to be filled. He was careful about the arrangements he made for you. Your father was very concerned about your safety and well-being"

"He cared as long as I was out of his way," she retorted.

"You know, we all get selfish at times and your pa was looking out for what he wanted first. That doesn't mean he loves you any the less. I guess we just have to learn to believe what the Bible tells us about all things working for good to those that love the Lord."

Delphinia picked up her cup and plate, slowly walked to the water's edge, and rinsed them off as Jonathan issued a silent prayer that God would help Delphinia forgive her father and find peace and happiness in her new home with them.

"We better get back. Mrs. Clauson said we should wash some clothes since we don't get many opportunities like this one," she remarked, walking past him.

Jonathan was still sitting and watching her as she moved toward the wagons when she turned and said, "I guess you weren't at fault, so my apology stands."

five

For the remainder of the day Delphinia was completely absorbed in her own thoughts. She wandered from one chore to another without realizing when she had begun one thing and ended another. After the evening meal, Jonathan led them in devotions and the moment the final "amen" had been uttered, Delphinia excused herself, anxious for the solitude the wagon would provide, even if only for an hour or two.

As Delphinia lay there, she began to pray. This prayer was different, however. It was not a request that God rescue her or that anything terrible happen to Mr. Wilshire. Rather, this prayer was that God give her the ability to forgive her father for deserting her and to grant her peace. Almost as an afterthought, she added that she could also use a bit of joy in her life. She fell asleep with that prayer on her lips.

Their few remaining days with the wagon train had passed in rapid succession when Jonathan advised her that the next day they would break away on their own. "I think the wagon master will be happy to see me leave. I've noticed it seems to upset him when folks look to me for leadership now that he's well again," he said with a grin.

"I think you may be right about that. I don't think some of the folks will look to him unless you're gone. They take to you more. Maybe it's because they view you as an answer to prayer," she responded.

"I hope I have been. Maybe someday I can be an answer to your prayers, too," he stated and then, noting her uneasiness, quickly changed the subject. "It's faster if we break off and head north on our own. We can make it home by evening without pushing too hard and it's safe, since the Indians around our area are pretty friendly. Besides, I've been gone quite a spell and I'm anxious to get home, if that's all right with you."

"Whatever you think is best," she replied, but suddenly a multitude of emotions began to envelope her. She was going to miss the Clausons and the other folks she had gotten to know on the train. She was frightened that Granny and the children would not accept her. And how, oh how, was she going to be able to take care of a houseful of children? The thought of such responsibility almost overwhelmed her. "Lord, please give me peace and joy and lots and lots of help," she quietly prayed.

The next morning they joined the Clausons for breakfast and Jonathan led them in a final prayer, while Delphinia attempted to remain calm. Mrs. Clauson hugged her close and whispered in her ear to be brave, which only served to heighten her level of anxiety. She forced a feeble smile, took up the reins, and bid the horses move out.

Delphinia found herself deep in thought as they made their way to the Wilshire homestead. Jonathan rode the mare, scouting ahead and then riding back to assure her all was well, not allowing much time for conversation. With each mile they traversed, she felt fear beginning to well up inside. As Jonathan came abreast of the wagon to tell her they would be home in about three hours, he noticed she was holding the reins with one hand and pressing down the pleats of her skirt in that slow, methodical motion he had come to recognize as a sign of uneasiness.

"This looks like it might be a good spot for us to stop for a short spell. I'm sure you could use a little rest and the horses won't mind, either," he remarked, hoping to give them a little time to talk and perhaps find out what was bothering her.

"I thought you wanted to keep moving. . .get home as early as possible. Isn't that what you've told me every time you rode back from scouting?" she asked, her voice sounding strained.

"You're right, I did say that," he commented as he reached across his mare and took hold of the reins, bringing the team and wagon to a halt. "But I think a short rest will do us both some good."

Climbing down from his horse, he tied it to the back of the wagon and then, walking to the side of the wagon, stretched his arms up to assist her down. As her feet touched the ground, Delphinia looked up and Jonathan was met by two of the saddest brown eyes he had ever seen. Instead of releasing her, he gathered her into his arms and held her, trying his best to give her comfort. Standing there with her in his arms, he realized he truly cared for this young woman.

Pushing away from him, Delphinia retorted, "I'm not a child anymore, Mr. Wilshire, so you needn't feel you have to stop and coddle me. I'll be fine, just fine," she said. Not wanting to ever again experience the pain of losing someone she cared about, Delphinia knew she would have to hold herself aloof.

"Is that what you think? That I feel you're a child who needs to be coddled? Well, believe me, Phiney, I know you're not a child, but I also know there isn't a soul who doesn't need comforting from time to time. . .even you."

Immediately, she regretted her abruptness but was not about to let down her defenses. Turning, she saw Jonathan walking down toward the dry creek bed below. Not sure what else to do, she followed along behind, trying to keep herself upright by grabbing at tree branches as the rocks underfoot began to slide.

"You sure wouldn't do well sneaking up on a person," he remarked without looking back.

"I wasn't trying to *sneak up* on you. I wanted to apologize for acting so precipitous. You've probably noticed that I sometimes lack the art of tactfulness. At least that's what Ma used to tell me on occasion."

When he did not respond, she looked at their surroundings and asked, "Is there some reason why you've come down here?"

"I guess I just wanted to look around. About two miles up this creek bed is where Sarah and Jake died. It's hard to believe, looking at it now."

"What do you mean by that? You never mentioned how they died. I thought they probably contracted some type of illness. Was it Indians?" she asked with a tremor in her voice.

Sitting down on a small boulder, he pulled a long piece of grass and tucked it between his teeth. "No, it wasn't illness or Indians that caused their death. It was a much-needed rain."

"I don't understand," she commented, coming up behind where he sat and making her way around the rock to sit next to him.

"I wasn't with them. Granny and I had stayed back at the farm. She hadn't been feeling herself and we needed supplies from town. Sarah hadn't been in town since the twins' birth and she was wanting to get a change of scenery and see folks. The children wanted to go along, too. Going to town is just about the next best thing to Christmas for the youngsters.

"So they got all loaded up, Sarah and Tessie each holding one of the twins and the boys all excited about showing off the babies and maybe getting a piece or two of candy. They packed a lunch thinking they'd stop on the way home and eat so Granny wouldn't have to prepare for them. We watched them pull out and Granny said she was going to have a cup of tea and rest a while so I went out to the barn to do some chores. The morning passed by uneventfully. I noticed some clouds gathering but didn't think much of it. We needed rain badly but every time storm clouds would appear, it seemed they'd pass us by and we'd be lucky to get a drop or two out of all the thunder and darkness.

"Granny and I just had some biscuits and cold meat for lunch and I told her I was going to move the livestock into the barn and pen up the chickens and hogs since it looked like a storm was headed our way. We always took precautions, figuring rain had to come behind some of those clouds one day.

"As it turned out, that was the day. It started with big, fat raindrops and I thought it was going to be another false alarm. But shortly, the animals started getting real skittish and it began to rain at a nice steady pace. I just stood there letting it wash over me it felt so good. I ran back to the cabin and Granny was standing on the porch, laughing and holding her hands out to feel that wonderful, much-needed rain. It must have been a full ten minutes we stood there in delight when all of a sudden, there was the loudest clap of thunder and a huge bolt of lightning. The skies appeared to just open up and pour water down so fast and hard I couldn't believe it.

"Granny and I got into the cabin as quick as we could when the downpour began and as soon as we got our senses about us thought of Jake, Sarah, and the children, praying they hadn't begun the trip home before the rain started. I think it was probably the longest time of my life, just waiting there. I couldn't leave to go search for them, knowing I could never make it through that downpour. It seemed it would never stop.

"It was the next day before it let up enough so I could travel at all. I started out with a few supplies and had to go slowly with the horse, the ground was so soaked. I wasn't sure which way Jake would be coming back from town, so I told Granny to pray that if they'd left town I'd choose the right direction. There are two ways for us to make it to town, and we usually didn't come by way of this creek bed. I was hoping that Jake hadn't chosen this, of all days, to come the creek bed route, but I felt led to start my search in this direction.

"The going was slow and rough and I became more and more frightened as I continued my search. I stopped at the Aplington's homestead but they hadn't seen anything of Jake and Sarah. After having a quick cup of coffee, I continued on toward the creek bed. . .or at least what had been a creek bed. It had turned into a virtual torrent of rushing water, limbs, and debris. As I looked down into that flood of water, I saw what I thought was one of the baskets Sarah used to carry the twins. I just stood there staring at the rushing water, completely out of its banks and roaring like a train engine, whipping that tiny basket back and forth.

"When I finally got my wits about me," he continued, "I knew I had to go farther upstream in hopes of finding the family. I tried to holler for them but the roar of the water drowned out my voice. I stayed as close to the creek as I could, hoping I'd see something to give me a clue about where they might be. I wasn't giving in to the fact that anything could have happened to any of them. Finally, after hours of searching, I stopped to pray and, as I finished my prayer, I looked up and spotted Tessie, waving a piece of Josh's shirt high in the air to get my attention. They were inside a small natural cave that had formed above the creek bed. I had no doubt the Lord had placed me in that spot so that when I looked up the first thing I would see was those children.

"I made my way up to them. They were in sad condition,

all of them. Not just being without food and water, but sick with worry and fear knowing their ma and pa were gone. That was a rough time I'd not like to go through again."

Delphinia stared fixedly at Jonathan as he related the story. It seemed he was almost in a trance as he recited the events. She reached over and placed her hand on his, but he didn't even seem to realize she was there. "What happened after you found them?"

"Even in the midst of all the sadness, the Lord provided. I had just managed to get two of the children down when Mr. Aplington and his older son arrived with a spring wagon. They worked with me until we had everyone down and loaded into the wagon.

"Tessie managed to tell us that Jake and Sarah were dead but it was much later before she was able to tell us what had happened. It seems that when the thunder and lightning started, the horses began to get excited. Jake decided to locate shelter and couldn't find any place to put them, except in that small cave. He went back down to try and get the horses and wagon to higher ground when a bolt of lightning hit, causing the horses to rear up and go out of control. They knocked him over and the wagon turned, landing on top of him. Sarah climbed back down, determined to get that wagon off of him, even though I'm sure he was already dead. Tessie said she screamed and screamed for her ma to come back up to them but she stayed there pushing and pushing, trying to get the wagon off Jake. When the water started rising, she tried to hold his head up, determined he was going to live.

"I imagine by the time she realized the futility of her efforts, the current was so strong there was no way she could make her way back. We found both of their bodies a few days later," his shoulders sagging as he finished relating the event.

"Oh, how awful for all of you. How those poor children ever managed to make it is truly a miracle," she said, having difficulty holding back the hot tears that threatened to spill over at any minute.

"You're right. It was God guiding my steps that caused me to find the children. I must admit, though, that the whole incident left some pretty deep scars on Tessie. The younger ones seem to have done better. Those poor little twins were so bedraggled and hungry by the time we got them back to the Aplingtons, I didn't ever expect them to pull through. The Lord provided for them, too, though. Mrs. Aplington had a goat she sent home with us and those twins took to that goat milk just like it was their mama's. Granny had me take the goat back just before I left to come for you. The twins seem to get along pretty well now with milk from old Josie, one of our cows, and food from the table, even if they are awful messy," he chuckled.

"I guess it's about time we get back to the wagon if we're going to get home before dark. Give me your hand and I'll help you back up the hill."

Several hours later, Delphinia spotted two cabins and looked questioningly at Jonathan who merely nodded his affirmance that they were home. Growing closer, Delphinia could make out several children standing on the porch, waving. Jonathan grinned widely at the sight of those familiar faces, and Delphinia felt a knot rise up in her stomach.

six

Jonathan reached up in his familiar stance to help Delphinia down from the wagon, and as she lowered herself into his arms, three sets of eyes peered at her from the porch. They were such handsome children!

Tessie was all Jonathan had described, and more. She had beautiful red hair and eyes of pale blue that seemed to flash with anger and then go dull. Josh and Joey were towheads with big blue eyes, like Jonathan. "Uncle Jon, Uncle Jon," called Joey. "Is this our new mama?"

"She's not our ma, Joey. Our ma is dead. No one can take Ma's place and don't you ever forget that," Tessie seethed back at the child.

"Mind your manners, young lady," Jonathan said, reaching down to lift Joey and swing him high in the air. "Joey, this is Phiney and she's come to help Granny and Tessie take care of you," he said, trying to soothe Tessie's outburst.

"And this is Joshua, the man of the house when I'm not around. You've already figured out who Tessie is," he said, giving an admonishing look to the redhead.

"Where are Granny and the twins?" he questioned the pouting girl.

"In the house. The twins are having supper early so we can enjoy the meal," Tessie remarked.

Jonathan laughed and grabbed Phiney's hand, pulling her through the doorway. "Granny, we've finally made it, let me introduce you to—"

"Delphinia Elizabeth Hughes," she interrupted.

Delphinia was met by a radiant smile, wisps of gray-white

47

hair, and a sparkling set of eyes amid creases and lines on a well-weathered face. "Delphinia, my dear, I am so pleased to have you with us. I have prayed daily for you and Jonathan, that your journey would be safe. You can't imagine how pleased I am that the Lord has sent you to be a part of our family," she beamed.

"Jonathan, we'll get dinner on the table soon. Hopefully the twins will have finished their mess before we're ready. Delphinia, let me show you where your room will be and Jon, bring her trunk in so she can get comfortable. Better get the horses put up, too, and might as well have Josh help you unload the wagon before we sit down to eat," she continued.

"Granny, I don't know how we made it back home without you telling us what to do and when to do it," Jonathan laughingly chided.

"Oh posh, just get going and do as I say. By tomorrow I'll probably be bedfast again and you can enjoy the peace and quiet."

Granny led Delphinia into a bedroom off the kitchen and she immediately knew it had belonged to Sarah and Jake. Judging from Tessie's critical looks, she surmised the room was regarded as sacred ground by the eldest child. Hoping to diffuse the situation, Delphinia requested a bed in the loft with the smaller children.

"The room is to be yours and I'll hear no more about it," the older woman insisted.

Delphinia placed her clothes in the drawers of the ornately carved chest and hung her dresses in the matching wardrobe, which had been brought from Ohio when Sarah and Jake had moved west. The room had been cleaned until it nearly shone; there was nothing left as a reminder that it had ever belonged to anyone else. Delphinia spread her quilt on the bed in coverlet fashion and placed her brush, mirror, and a picture of her parents on the chest in an attempt to make the room feel more like home. She had just about completed her unpacking, when she saw Tessie standing in the doorway, peering into the room.

"Why don't you come in and join me while I finish?" Delphinia offered.

"I like your quilt," Tessie ventured, slowly entering the room.

"Why, thank you. It's a precious treasure to me. My mama and I made this quilt before she died. I don't think my mother ever thought I'd get it finished. She spent lots of hours teaching me how to make the different stitches until they met her inspection. I wasn't much older than you when I started making the quilt. Mama told me quilts were sewn with threads of love. I thought it must have been threads of patience because they took so long to make. Especially the ones Mama supervised! She was a real stickler for perfect stitches," she laughed.

"I've found great comfort having it since my mother died and through the journey here, it was like I was bringing a part of her with me, more than a picture or piece of jewelry, because her hands helped sew those threads that run through the quilt. I'm not near as good as she was, but if you'd like to make a quilt, perhaps we could find some old pieces of cloth and I could help you," she offered.

Overhearing their conversation, Granny commented, "Why, Sarah had started a quilt top last winter and I'll bet it's around here somewhere, Tessie. We'll see if we can find it and you and Delphinia can finish it. Once winter sets in, it'll be a good project for the two of you."

"No, I'm not making any quilt, not this winter, not ever, and I don't want her touching Mama's quilt, either," Tessie hastened to add, her voice full of anger.

Not wanting to upset the girl, Delphinia smiled and moved into the kitchen to assist with dinner. Shortly, they were all around a table laden with wonderful food and conversation. Granny told them she had been sure they would arrive home that very day, which was why she and Tessie had prepared a special dinner of chicken and dumplings. Delphinia was quick to tell both women the meal was as good as anything she had ever tasted. The children tried to talk all at once, telling Jonathan of the happenings since his departure. All but Tessie. She remained sullen and aloof, speaking only when necessary.

After dinner while they sat visiting, Delphinia watched as Nettie crawled toward her with a big grin. Attempting to pull herself up, she looked at Delphinia and babbled, "Mama." No sooner had she uttered the word than Tessie became hysterical, screaming to the infant that her mama was dead. Startled, Nettie lost her balance and toppled backward, her head hitting the chair as she fell. Reaching down, Delphinia lifted the crying child into her arms, cooing and rocking in an attempt to soothe her.

"Give her to me! She's my sister," Tessie fumed.

"Leave her be. You march yourself outside right now," Jonathan instructed, his voice cold and hard.

Delphinia did not miss the expressions of hatred and enmity that crossed Tessie's face as she walked toward the door. They were embedded in her memory. When Jonathan and Tessie returned a short time later, she apologized, but Delphinia and Tessie both knew it came only from her lips, not her heart. The child's pain was obvious to everyone, including Delphinia, for she, too, knew the pain of losing parents.

Lying in bed that night and comparing her loss to Tessie's, she realized the Lord had answered her prayers. She no longer was harboring the resentment for her pa and feeling sorry for herself. It had happened so subtly she hadn't even discerned it, and the realization amazed her. She slipped out of bed and knelt down beside her bed, thanking God for an answer to her prayers and then petitioning Him to help Tessie as He had helped her.

"Please, Lord," she prayed, "give me the knowledge to help this girl find some peace." She crawled back into bed and the next thing she heard were noises in the kitchen and the sound of the twins' babbling voices.

Jumping out of bed she quickly dressed, pulled her hair back, and tied it with a ribbon at the nape of her neck. *I'll put it up later when there's more time,* she decided. Rushing to the kitchen, she was met by Granny's smiling face and the twins' almost toothless grins.

"I'm so sorry. I must have overslept. I'm usually up quite early. You can ask Mr. Wilshire. Even on the wagon train, I was almost always up before the others," she blurted without pausing for breath.

"You needn't get so excited, child. Jonathan said to let you sleep late. He knew you were tired, as did I. There's no need to be upset. When I'm feeling well enough I always get up with the twins and fix Jonathan's breakfast. I usually let the others sleep until after he's gone to do his chores. That way we get to visit with a little peace and quiet. Jonathan and I both enjoy having a short devotion time in the morning before we start the day and I hope you'll join us for that," she continued. "One other thing, Delphinia, *please* quit calling Jonathan *Mr. Wilshire.* Either call him Jonathan or Jon, I don't care which, but not Mr. Wilshire. We don't stand on formality around here, and you're a part of this family now. I want you to call me Granny just like every other member of this family and I'll call you Delphinia. Jonathan tells me your name is very important to you. Now then, let's wake up the rest of the family and get this day going," she said. "I'll let you have the honor of climbing to the loft and rousing the children," she said, moving to set the table.

ᐓ

Delphinia could not believe the way the day was flying by. Granny seemed to have enough energy for two people. Leaning over a tub of hot water, scrubbing a pair of work pants, Delphinia commented that she did not understand why anyone felt that the older woman needed help.

"Well, child," Granny answered, "right now I'm doing just fine, and I have been this past week or so. But shortly after Jon left for Illinois, I had a real setback. Course this has been happening more and more lately. Jonathan made arrangements for Katy McVay to come stay if I had trouble. I sent Josh down to Aplington's place and Ned Aplington went to town and fetched Katy for me. She's a nice girl. Not a whole lot of sense and doesn't know how to do as much as some around the house, but she's good with the young children. Course, Tessie helped a lot, too. Once I got to feeling better, I sent Katy back home. Her folks run the general store in town and they need her there to help out, so I didn't want to keep her longer than necessary."

Tessie was hanging the clothes on a rope tied between two small trees, intently listening to the conversation of the older women as they performed their chores.

"Katy's got her cap set for Uncle Jon. That's why she wanted to come over to help out," Tessie injected into the conversation, with a smirk on her face. "I think he's sweet on her, too, 'cause Katy told me they were going to the basket dinner after church next week. He's probably going to ask her to marry him," she said, watching Delphinia for a reaction.

Delphinia wasn't sure why, but she felt a dull ache in the pit of her stomach.

"Tessie, I don't know where you get such notions," Granny scolded. "I sometimes think you must lie awake at night, dreamin' up some of these stories. If Jonathan was of a mind to marry Katy, I think someone besides you and Katy would know about it."

"Did I hear my name?" Jonathan asked as he came striding up from the barn, a bucket of milk in each large hand.

"Oh, Tessie's just going on about Katy having her cap set for you and telling us you two have plans to get married. How come you're carrying that milk up here? I thought Josh would have brought it up hours ago," Granny replied.

"Think he must have his mind on something besides his chores today. I told him he could go do some fishing at the pond when he finished milking since he worked so hard while I was gone. Seems he forgot that bringing the buckets up to the house is part of milking. Besides, I don't mind doing it, but I'm sure you women can find something better to talk about than my love life," he chuckled.

Not wanting to miss an opportunity to put Delphinia in her place, Tessie said in an almost syrupy voice, "But Uncle Jon, Katy said you had asked her to the church picnic. Everyone knows you're sweet on each other."

"Well, Tessie, I don't think you've got the story quite right, which is what usually comes of idle gossip. In any event, Katy asked me if I'd escort her to the church dinner and I told her I didn't know if I would be back in time. I feel sure she's made other arrangements by now, and I'm planning on all of us attending as a family. Why don't you get out to the chicken coop and see about collecting eggs instead of spreading gossip?" he ordered as he continued toward the house.

seven

The following days were filled with endless chores and wonderful conversations with Granny. Her love of the Lord caused her to nearly glow all the time. She could quote Scriptures for almost any situation, and then she would smile and say, "Praise God, I may not be as strong as when I was young, but I've still got my memory." That statement never ceased to make Delphinia grin.

Delphinia felt as if she had known Granny all her life and a closeness emerged that she had not felt since her mama died. Kneeling at her bed each night, Delphinia thanked God for the older woman and all she was teaching her about life and survival in the West, but most of all, how to love God and find joy in any circumstance.

Sunday morning found Delphinia musing about mornings long ago when she would rise and have only herself to clothe and care for. How things had changed! Granny advised her to dress the twins last, since they always managed to get themselves dirty if given an opportunity. Jonathan had already loaded the baskets of food and everyone was waiting in the wagon. With great care, she placed a tiny ribbon around Nettie's head, lifted her off the bed, and walked out to join them.

Jonathan jumped down to help her, a wide grin on his face. "I think Nettie's more prone to eating hair ribbons than wearing them," he laughed, pulling the ribbon out of the baby's chubby fist and handing it to Delphinia. Smiling, she gave a sigh and placed the ribbon in her pocket.

The twins slept through most of the church service with

Jonathan holding Nathan and Nettie snuggled in Delphinia's arms. Tessie made sure she was seated between the two of them. Josh and Joey were on either side of Granny, who managed to keep their fidgeting to a minimum by simply patting a hand on occasion.

After services, Granny tugged Delphinia along, telling her she wanted to introduce the pastor before they unloaded the wagon. Granny presented her to Pastor Martin and continued with a recitation about all of her fine qualities until Delphinia was embarrassed to even look at him. She merely extended her hand and mumbled, "Pleased to meet you. I think I better change Nettie's diaper."

Turning to make her getaway, she nearly collided with Jonathan, who was visiting with a beautiful young woman.

"Delphinia, I'd like you to meet Katy McVay," he said as they walked along beside her to the wagon.

Just as they rounded the corner of the church, Tessie appeared. "Oh, Katy, please join us for lunch. It won't be any fun without you," she pleaded.

"Well, if you *all* want me to, I couldn't refuse," Katy responded, smiling demurely as she looped her arm through Jonathan's.

Jonathan wasn't quite sure how to handle the turn of events and looked from Katy to Delphinia. His eyes finally settled on Tessie who was beaming with her accomplishment but quickly looked away when she noted her uncle's glare.

Watching the unfolding events from her position just outside the church, Granny decided to invite the young pastor to join them and share their meal. Realizing Tessie was enjoying the uncomfortable situation she had created, Granny assigned her the task of caring for the twins and Joey after dinner. Josh was off playing games with the other young boys, while the adults visited with several other families.

Delphinia was introduced to everyone as the newest member of the Wilshire household and the afternoon passed all too quickly when Jonathan announced it was time to load up and head for home.

Delphinia took note that Katy was still following after Jonathan like a lost puppy. Smiling inwardly, she wondered if Katy would climb in the wagon with the rest of the family—not that she cared, of course. Jonathan could spend his time with whomever he chose, she thought to herself.

Granny organized the children in the back of the wagon, firmly plopped Nettie and Nate in Tessie's lap, and waited until Delphinia was seated. She then ordered Jonathan to help her to the front, telling him she wished to visit with Delphinia on the return trip. Delphinia slid to the middle of the seat and once Jonathan had hoisted himself into place, the three of them were sandwiched together in much closer proximity than Katy McVay would have preferred. With mounting displeasure the young woman stood watching the group but tried to keep her composure by saying, "Be sure and put that shawl around your shoulders, Granny. It's getting chilly."

"Not to worry, Katy," smiled the older woman, a twinkle in her eye. "We'll keep each other warm. You better run along before your folks miss you." The dismissal was apparent as Granny turned to Delphinia and began to chat.

"It sure was a fine day. I don't think I've gotten to visit with so many folks since Zeb and Ellie got married last year. I'm glad you got to meet everyone so soon after your arrival, Delphinia. You probably won't remember all their names, but the faces will be familiar and it makes you feel more at home when you see a friendly face," Granny commented. "Pastor Martin seemed mighty impressed with you, I might add."

Jonathan let out a grunt to her last remark and although Delphinia did not comment, Jonathan saw a slight blush rise in her cheeks and a smile form on her lips.

"It seemed to me you were pretty impressed with Pastor Martin yourself, Phiney," Jonathan bantered. "Every time I saw you, you were at his side."

Delphinia felt herself bristle at his remark. Why, he made it sound like she had been throwing herself at the pastor. She, with two tiny babies to diaper and feed, while he was off squiring Miss Katy McVay, fixing her a plate of food, carrying her parasol like it belonged to him, and making a total fool of himself. She all but bit her tongue off trying to remain in control.

"You might as well say what's on your mind 'fore you bust a button, Phiney. I can see you've got a whole lot of things you're just itching to say," he goaded.

Glancing over her shoulder, she observed the children were asleep. Looking at him with those same fiery eyes he had seen at the general store before he brought her west, he felt a strong urge to gather her into his arms and hold her close. Instead, he listened as she went into a tirade about how Katy McVay had been attached to him like another appendage and how foolish he had looked carrying her parasol.

"Well, I thank you for your insights, *Miss Hughes*," he responded as he lifted her down from the wagon and firmly placed her on the ground, "but I doubt I looked any more foolish than you did prancing behind Pastor Martin. I'm surprised you didn't ask to carry his Bible."

"How could I?" she retorted. "I was too busy carrying your nephew most of the time." With that said, she turned and carried Nathan into the cabin without so much as a good night. *I'm not going to let myself care for any man,* she thought to herself. *I've forgiven Pa for sending me away, but I've not forgotten. I don't need that kind of pain ever again.*

"My, my," smiled Granny as she gathered the other children and walked toward the cabin. "You two certainly have hit it off well. I'm so pleased."

Jonathan stood staring after her, wondering if she had lost her senses.

❧

Life began to fit into a routine for the family and although Delphinia still relied on Granny for many things, Granny had fewer and fewer days when she was up and about for any period of time. Jonathan made a bed for her to lie on in the living area so she could be in the midst of things. Granny still led them in devotions each morning and continued to be a stabilizing factor for Tessie, whose resentment of Delphinia seemed immeasurable. Everyone else was accepting Delphinia's presence and enjoying her company, particularly Pastor Martin.

It was a warm day and Delphinia had risen early, hoping to get the bread baking done before the heat of the day made the cabin unbearable. Her back was to the door as she stood kneading the coarse dough, methodically punching and turning the mixture, her thoughts occasionally drifting to Pastor Martin's good looks and kind manner. This was the last batch of dough and she was glad it would soon be done. She could feel droplets of perspiration forming across her forehead when she heard Granny say from the narrow cot, "Delphinia, don't be alarmed and don't scream. Just slowly turn around and smile like this is the happiest moment of your life."

Not knowing what to expect, the younger woman whirled around to be greeted by three Indians who were solemnly staring at her as her mouth fell open and she began moving backward.

"Smile, Delphinia, smile," Granny commanded.

"I'm trying, Granny, I'm honestly trying, but I can't seem to get my lips to turn upward right now. What do they want? Is Jonathan anywhere nearby?"

"Oh, they're friendly enough and they belong to the Kansa tribe. Just don't act like you're afraid. It offends them since they've come here from time to time and have never hurt anyone. They seem to know the days when I bake bread and that's what they want. I thought they had moved to the reservation, it's been so long since they've been here. They used to come every week or two and expect a loaf of bread and maybe some cheese or a chicken. Then they just quit coming. They never knock, just walk in and stand there until they're noticed. Gives you quite a start the first time, though.

"You want bread?" Granny asked, pointing at the freshly baked loaves resting on the wooden table.

Nodding in the affirmative, they each reached out and grabbed a loaf of bread.

"Now just a minute," Delphinia chastened. "You can't each have a loaf. You'll have to settle for one loaf. I have children here to feed."

"Well you lost your fear mighty fast, child," Granny commented as she looked over to see both twins toddling into the kitchen.

"You papoose?" one of the Indians asked, pointing first at Delphinia and then the twins, seeming amazed at the sight of them.

"They haven't been here since the twins were born," Granny commented. "I don't know if they realize you're not Sarah, but just nod yes."

"Yes, my papoose," Delphinia said, pointing to herself and to each of the twins while the Indians walked toward the babies, looking at them curiously. Then, reaching down, the spokesman picked up Nettie in one arm and Nathan in the other. He began bouncing the babies as he talked and laughed with his companions. Both infants were enthralled with the attention and were busy stuffing the Indian's necklaces into their mouths.

Delphinia glanced at the older woman and knew she was becoming alarmed by the Indian's interest in the babies.

Forgetting her fear, she walked to the Indian and said, "My papoose," and extended her arms. Grunting in agreement, the Indian passed the children to her, picked up a loaf of bread, held it in the air, and the three of them left the cabin without saying another word.

"Wow," said Josh, coming from behind the bedroom door. "You sure were brave."

"Yeah, brave," mimicked Joey.

"I don't know about brave," Delphinia answered, "but they were making me terribly nervous and I was afraid they'd walk out with more than a loaf of bread."

Jonathan was just coming over from his cabin when he was met by Joey and Josh, both trying to give an account of everything that had happened, even though they had witnessed very little of the actual events.

"Slow down, you guys, or I'll never be able to understand. Better yet, why don't you let Granny or Phiney tell me what happened."

Joint "ahs" emitted from both boys at that suggestion and they plopped down on the bed with Granny as she began to tell Jonathan what had occurred.

"Seems you finally put that temper of yours to good use, Phiney," Jonathan responded after hearing Granny's account of what had happened.

"I what? Well, of all the—"

"Now, now child," Granny interrupted, "he's just trying to get you riled up, and doing a mighty fine job of it, too, I might add. Pay him no mind. He's as proud of you as the rest of us."

"She's right, Phiney. I should be thanking you instead of teasing. That was mighty brave of you and we're grateful although I can't say as I blame those Indians for wanting some of Granny's bread. Those are some fine looking loaves."

"They're not mine, Jonathan. I couldn't begin to knead

that bread the way I've been feeling. Delphinia's baked all the bread around here for weeks now."

"Well, I think Granny's bread is much better, and so was Mama's," came Tessie's response from the other side of the room. "I don't know why you're making such a big fuss. Those Indians weren't going to hurt anyone. They were just curious about the twins and wanted a handout. She's no big deal. We've had Indians in and out of this cabin before she ever came here."

"You're right, Tessie. I'm sure the Indians meant no harm and I did nothing the rest of you wouldn't have done. So let's just forget it and get breakfast going. Tessie, if you'll start more coffee, I believe I'll go to my room for a few minutes and freshen up."

Once inside her room, Delphinia willed herself to stop shaking. Leaning against the closed door, her ghostlike reflection greeted her in the bureau mirror. Aware the family was waiting breakfast and not wanting to appear faint-hearted, she pinched her cheeks, forced a smile on her face, and walked back to the kitchen realizing she had been thanking God from the instant the Indians left the cabin until this moment. Immediately, she felt herself quit shivering and a peaceful calm took the place of her fear.

Granny's supplication at the morning meal was more eloquent than usual and Jonathan was quick to add a hearty "amen" on several occasions throughout the prayer. Delphinia silently thanked God for the peace He had granted her. She was not aware until this day that some time ago she had quit praying for God to rescue her and had allowed laughter and joy to return to her life. It was not the same as when she had been at home with her parents, but a warmth and love of a new and special kind had slowly begun to grow in her heart.

eight

Autumn arrived and the trees burst forth in glorious yellows, reds, and oranges. The rolling hills took on a new beauty and Delphinia delighted in the changing season. The warm air belied the fact that winter would soon follow.

For several days Josh and Joey had been hard at work, gathering apples from the surrounding trees, stripping them of the tart, crisp fruit. An ample supply had been placed in the root cellar and she and Granny had spent days drying the rest. Hoping she might find enough to make pies for dessert that evening, Delphinia had gone to the trees in the orchard behind the house. Once the basket was full, she started back toward the cabin and, when coming around the house, she noticed Pastor Martin riding toward her on his sorrel. Waving in recognition, he came directly to where she stood, dismounted, and joined her.

"I was hoping to catch you alone for a minute," he commented as he walked beside her, leading the horse. "I've come to ask if you'd accompany me to the social next Friday evening," he blurted, "unless you're going with Jonathan. . . or has someone else already asked you?"

Before she could answer, Tessie came around the side of the house, a twin at each hand. "You'd better take him up on the offer, Phiney. Jonathan will be taking Katy McVay, and I doubt *you'll* be getting any other invitations," a malicious smile crossing her face.

"I don't know if I'll be attending at all, Pastor Martin. I had quite forgotten about the party and I'm not sure I can leave the family. Granny hasn't been quite as good the last few days."

"Really, Phiney. We're not totally helpless, you know. We managed before you got here and I'm sure we could manage for a few hours on Friday night," came Tessie's rebuttal.

Not sure whether she should thank Tessie for the offer to assist with the family or upbraid her for her rude intrusion, Delphinia invited the pastor to join her in the cabin where they could discuss the matter further and gain Granny's opinion.

Granny was always pleased to see Pastor Martin and her face shone immediate pleasure as he walked in the room. "I didn't know you made calls this early in the day," she called out in greeting.

Smiling, he sat in the chair beside the bed where she rested and he took her hand. "Normally I don't and only for very special occasions. I've come to ask Delphinia if she'd allow me to escort her to the social Friday night," he answered, accepting the cup of coffee Delphinia offered.

"Well, I'd say that's a pretty special event. What kind of answer did you give this young man, Delphinia?" she asked the embarrassed young woman.

"I haven't answered him just yet, Granny. I didn't think I should leave the children with you for that long. Tessie overheard the conversation and said she could help but I wanted to talk it over with you first."

"Why, we can manage long enough for you to have a little fun, Delphinia. Wouldn't want you away too long, though. I'd miss your company and sweet face."

Delphinia leaned down to place a light kiss on the older woman's wrinkled cheek. "I love you, Granny," she whispered.

"Does that mean you've accepted?" asked Tessie, coming from the doorway where she had been standing out of sight and listening.

"Well. . .yes. . .I suppose it does," she replied. "Pastor Martin, I'd be pleased to accompany you. What time should I be ready?"

"I'll be here about seven, if that's agreeable."

Glancing over at Granny for affirmation and seeing her nod, Delphinia voiced her agreement.

Downing the remains of coffee in the stoneware cup, the young parson bid them farewell, explaining he needed to stop by the Aplingtons' for a visit and get back to town before noon. Walking outside, Delphinia strolled along beside him until he had come even with his mare. "If you're going to attend the social with me, Delphinia, I think it would be appropriate for you to call me George," he stated and swung atop the animal, which was prancing, anxious to be allowed its rein.

"Fine, George," she answered modestly, stepping back from the horse.

Smiling, he lightly kicked the mare in the sides and took off, reaching full gallop before he hit the main road, his arm waving in farewell.

Delphinia was standing in the same spot when Jonathan came up behind her and eyed the cloud of billowing dust down the road. Unable to identify the rider, he asked, "Who was that just leaving?"

"Jonathan, you frightened me. I didn't hear you come up behind me," she said, not answering his question.

"I'm sorry if I startled you. Who did you say that was, or is it a secret?"

"I didn't say, but it's not a secret. It was George. . .I mean, Pastor Martin."

"Oh, *George,* is it? Since when are you and the parson on a first name basis, Phiney?"

"Pastor Martin. . .George. . .has asked me to attend the social with him on Friday night," she responded.

"You didn't agree, did you?" His anger evident, the look on his face almost defied her to admit her acceptance.

"I checked with Granny. She found no fault in my going. I'll make sure the twins and Joey are ready for bed before leaving, if that's your concern." Irritated by the tone he was taking, Delphinia turned and headed back toward the house, leaving him to stare after her.

"Just you wait a minute. I'm not through discussin' this," he called after her.

"You needn't bellow. I didn't realize we were having a discussion. I thought it was an inquisition," she stated, continuing toward the house. *Why is he acting so hateful?* she wondered. *Jonathan knows George Martin is a good man. He should be pleased that such a nice man wants to keep company with me.*

"The problem is that I planned on taking you to the social and here you've gone and promised to go with George," he retorted.

Stopping short, she whirled around almost colliding with him. "You planned on taking me? Well, just when were you going to tell me about it? This is the first time you've said one word about the social. Besides, Tessie said you were taking Katy McVay."

"Tessie said what?" he nearly yelled at her. "Since when do you listen to what Tessie has to say?"

"Why wouldn't I believe her? I've heard enough rumors that you and Katy are a match. She's got her cap set for you and from what I've been told, the feeling is mutual," she retorted.

"Oh, really? Well, I don't pay much heed to the gossip that's floating around. For your information, we are not a *match*. I've escorted Katy to a few functions but that doesn't make us betrothed or anything near it. If Tessie told you I invited Katy, she spoke out of turn. I've not asked anyone to the social because I planned on taking you."

"I can't read your mind, Jonathan. If you want me to know what you're planning, next time you need to tell me," she answered, his comments making her more certain that men were not to be trusted.

The kitchen was filled with an air of tension throughout the noon meal until Granny finally questioned Jonathan. Hearing his explanation, she let out a whoop and sided with Delphinia. "Just because she lives here doesn't mean you can take her for granted," she chided.

Feeling frustration with Granny's lack of allegiance, Jonathan turned on Tessie, scolding her mightily for interfering.

"That's enough, Jon. I know you're upset, and the girl was wrong in telling an outright lie, but all your ranting and raving isn't going to change the fact that the preacher is calling on Delphinia Friday night," Granny resolutely stated.

Not willing to let the matter rest and hoping to aid Katy in her conquest, Tessie suggested Jonathan ride into town and invite her. "I'm sure she'll not accept an invitation from anyone else," she added as her final comment.

"Tessie, I would appreciate it if you would spend as much time performing chores as you do meddling in other people's affairs. If you'd do that, the rest of us wouldn't have to do a thing around here!" His face was reddened with anger as he pushed away from the table and left the house.

᠅

When Friday evening finally arrived, Granny made sure that Josh fetched water and it was kept warm on the stove for Delphinia's bath. After dinner, she ordered Jonathan to carry the metal tub into Delphinia's room, then smiled to herself as Jonathan made a dash for his own cabin to prepare for the evening.

Scooting down in the tub, Delphinia let her head go completely underwater and, sliding back up, began to lather her hair. She rubbed in a small amount of the lavender oil that had belonged to her mother and finished washing herself. Never had she taken such care in preparing herself. She towel dried her hair and pinned it on top of her head. An ivory ribbon surrounded the mass of curls except for a few short tendrils that escaped, framing her oval face. Her mother's small, golden locket was at her neck and she placed a tiny gold earring in each lobe.

She had decided upon wearing a deep blue dress that had belonged to her mother. Granny helped with the few necessary alterations and it now fit beautifully. She slipped it over her head and fastened the tiny covered buttons that began at the scooped neckline and trailed to the waist. Slipping on her good shoes, she took one final look in the mirror and exited the bedroom.

Her entry into the living area was met with lusty approval from the boys. Granny beamed at the sight of her and Tessie glared in distaste. Jonathan had gone to sit on the porch when he heard the raves from inside. Rising, he entered the house and was overcome by the sight he beheld. She was, without a doubt, the most glorious looking creature he had ever seen. Noting the look on his face, Tessie stepped toward him. "Aren't you leaving to pick up Katy, Uncle Jon?"

Gaining his attention with her question, he looked her straight in the eyes. "I told you earlier this week I was not escorting Katy. Have you forgotten, Tessie?"

"Oh, I thought maybe you'd asked her since then," she murmured. Gathering her wits about her, she quizzed, "Well, who are you taking?"

"No one," he responded, unable to take his eyes off the beautiful young woman in the blue dress. "I'm just going to ride along with George and Phiney."

"You're going to *what*?" stammered Delphinia.

"No need in getting my horse all lathered up riding into

town when there's a buggy going anyway. Doesn't make good sense, Phiney. Besides, I'm sure the parson won't mind if I ride along."

No sooner had he uttered those words, when the sound of a buggy could be heard coming up the roadway. Jonathan stepped to the porch and called out, "Evenin', George. Good to see you. I was just telling Phiney I didn't think you'd have any objection to my riding into town with the two of you. Didn't see any need to saddle up my horse when I could ride along with you."

The pastor's face registered a look of surprise and then disappointment. "No, no, that's fine, Jon. Might be a little crowded—"

"Don't mind a bit," interrupted Jonathan. "You just stay put and I'll fetch Phiney.

"I think perhaps I should fetch her myself, Jon," his voice hinting of irritation.

Both men arrived at the door simultaneously and for a moment Delphinia thought they were going to be permanently wedged in the doorway until the pastor turned slightly, allowing himself to advance into the room. "You look absolutely stunning, Delphinia," he complimented, watching her cheeks flush from the remark.

"She's a real sight to behold, that's for sure," responded Jonathan as every eye in the room turned to stare at him.

Nate and Nettie toddled to where she stood, their hands extended to grab at the flowing gown. "No you don't, you two. Tessie, grab the twins or they'll be drooling all over her before she can get out the door," ordered Jonathan.

"Seems to me you're already drooling all over her," Tessie muttered under her breath.

❧

The evening passed in a succession of dances with Jonathan and George vying for each one, occasionally being bested by some other young man who would manage to whisk her off in the midst of their sparring over who should have the next dance. By the end of the social, Delphinia's feet ached but the gaiety of the event far outweighed any complaint she might have. The only blemish of the evening had been overhearing some unkind remarks from Katy McVay at the refreshment table. When she noticed Delphinia standing close by, she had given her a syrupy smile and excused herself to "find more appealing company."

Although they were cramped close together on the seat of the buggy, the autumn air had cooled and Delphinia felt herself shiver. "You're cold. Why didn't you say something? Let me help you with your shawl," Jonathan offered as the pastor kept his hands on the reins. Unfolding the wrap, he slipped it around her shoulders and allowed his arm to rest across her shoulders in a possessive manner. Much to George's irritation, he remained thus until the horses came to a halt in front of the house. Jumping down, George hurried to secure the horses in hopes of helping Delphinia from the buggy, but to no avail. Jonathan had already assisted her and was standing with his arm draped across her small shoulders. Delphinia attempted to shrug him off but he only tightened his grip.

"It's getting late, Parson, and you've still got to make the trip back to town. Thanks for the ride and good night," Jonathan stated, attempting to dismiss the preacher before he could usher Delphinia to the house.

"Now just a minute, Jonathan. I'm capable of saying thank you and good night for myself. You go on to your place. George and I will be just fine," Delphinia answered.

"Nah, that's okay. Want to make sure everything's okay here before I go over to my place so I'll just wait here on the porch till George is on his way."

Knowing that Jonathan was not about to leave and not

wanting to create a scene, the pastor thanked Delphinia for a lovely evening and bid them both good night.

"Of all the nerve," she shouted at the relaxed figure on the porch. "You are the most vexing man I have ever met. George Martin made a trip here especially to invite me to the social, made another trip to escort me and return me safely home, and you have the nerve to not only invite yourself along, but won't even give him the opportunity to spend a moment alone with me!" The full moon shone on her face and he could see her eyes flashing with anger.

"I'll not apologize for that, Phiney. After all, I have a responsibility to keep you safe. You're a part of this family," he said with a boyish grin.

Hands on her hips and chin jutted forward, she made her way to the porch where he stood and she said, "I'll have you know, *Mr. Wilshire,* that I do not need your protection from George Martin, nor do I want it."

But, before she could move, he leaned down and kissed her full on the mouth. When he released her she was so stunned that she stared at him in utter disbelief, unable to say a word, her heart pounding rapidly. A slow smile came across his lips as he once again gathered her into his arms and his mouth slowly descended and captured her lips in a breathtaking kiss. She felt her legs grow limp and, as he leaned back, she lost her balance causing her to reach out and grab Jonathan's arm for support.

"Now, now, Phiney, don't go begging me to stay any longer. I've got to get over to my place and get some sleep," he said with an ornery glint in his eye.

That remark caused Delphinia to immediately regain her composure. "Beg you to stay? Is that what you think I want? Why, you are the most conceited, arrogant, irritating, interfering—"

"You just keep on with your chattering, Phiney. Think I'll

get some sleep," he interrupted, stepping off the porch and walking toward his cabin.

"Oooh, that man! I don't think the Lord is ever going to get around to straightening him out," she muttered under her breath as she turned and opened the cabin door.

nine

The beginning of the school year brought excitement to the household and the children were anxious for the change in routine. Delphinia made sure that each of the youngsters looked their very best for the first day, especially Joey, since this marked the beginning of his career as a student. Although he was not yet five, the new schoolteacher had come to visit and, much to his delight, declared him bright enough to begin his formal education with the other children. Delphinia and Granny packed their tin pails with thick slices of bread and cheese, an apple, and a piece of dried peach pie. The two women stood at the cabin door watching as the young Wilshires made their way toward the dusty road, their happy chatter floating through the morning air.

With the older children gone to school each day, Delphinia and Granny were left at home with only the twins to care for. Although she loved all the children, even Tessie with her malicious ways, Delphinia cherished the additional time it allowed her to be alone with the older woman.

Granny took advantage of the new-found freedom and devoted most of the extra hours to teaching Delphinia all the things that would assist the young woman in running the household once she had only herself to rely upon. Shortly after her arrival, Delphinia confided that her mother had given her a wonderful education, insisting she spend her time studying, reading, and doing fancy stitching rather than household tasks. It was soon evident that she had much to learn. During the months since her arrival, she had proven herself a capable student of the older woman's tutelage. But there remained much to learn and Granny spent hours carefully explaining how to use the children's clothing to make patterns for new garments; how to plant and tend a garden; how to preserve the meats, vegetables, and fruits that would provide for them throughout the winter and early spring; how to make tallow candles and lye soap, being sure to wrap each candle and bar in straw for storage; how to make big wheels of cheese, being sure to allow time for aging; and how to prepare meals for the large, threshing crews that would hopefully be needed in early summer. Listening intently, she absorbed everything Granny taught her.

Delphinia's true pleasure came, however, when Granny would call for a quiet time during the twins' nap and the two of them would read from the Bible and discuss the passages. Their sharing of God's Word caused a bond of love to flourish between the two women, just as the one that had grown between Delphinia and her mother when they stitched her cherished quilt. Both women were especially pleased when Pastor Martin would stop by, which was happening more frequently. He never failed to raise their spirits. Delphinia enjoyed his attentiveness and insights, while Granny hoped the visits would light a fire under Jonathan.

As winter began to settle on the prairie, Delphinia thought she would never see a blade of grass or a flower bloom again. The snows came in blizzard proportions, keeping the children, as well as the adults, inside most of the time. Although everyone made great effort to create harmony, boredom overcame the children and tempers grew short.

After several days, Delphinia was sure something would have to be done to keep the children diverted. That evening as Jonathan prepared to go to the barn and milk Josie, their old brown and white cow, Delphinia began putting on her coat and hat. "Where do you think you're going?" he asked. "I want to go to the barn and unpack some things from one of my trunks stored out there," she answered, falling in step behind him.

Barely able to see, the snow blowing in giant swirls with each new gust of wind, they made their way to the barn and, while Jonathan milked, Delphinia began going through the items in one of her trunks. She found her old slate and schoolbooks, an old cloth ball, a rag doll from when she was a small child, and some marbles her father had bought for her one Christmas, much to her mother's chagrin. She bundled the items in a heavy shawl and sat down on top of the trunk to await Jonathan.

"Come sit over here and visit with me while I finish," he requested.

Picking up the parcel, she walked over and sat on one of the milking stools, watching intently as the milk pinged into the battered pail at a steady rhythm.

"Granny tells me George has been coming out to see you some."

"He's been here occasionally."

"I take it that makes you happy?" Jonathan questioned, noting the blush that had risen in her cheeks.

"George is a fine man. I enjoy his company. And what of Katy McVay? Do your visits with her make you happy?" she questioned.

"I haven't been visiting with Katy. I don't know how I've missed George when he's come calling," he replied, rising from the stool. "Guess I need to be a little more observant," he grumbled as the two of them headed back toward the house.

"From the looks of that bundle, it appears your trip was successful," Granny said, watching the children assemble around Delphinia who was struggling to remove her wet outer garments.

"Perhaps more successful than the children will care for in

a few days," she answered with a slight smile, pointing at the teaching materials she was removing from the shawl. Handing the rag doll to Nettie, she smiled as the baby hugged it close and toddled away, with Nate in close pursuit.

"Here Nathan, catch the ball," she called, just as he was reaching to pull the doll away from Nettie. Chortling in delight, he grabbed the ball with his chubby hands as it rolled across the floor in front of him.

"Where are our toys?" asked Josh, a frown crossing his face.

"I don't have a lot of toys, Josh," she replied. "I do have some marbles my pa gave me one Christmas that I'd be willing to let you boys earn by doing well with your lessons."

"Ah, that's not fair," they replied in unison. "The twins don't have to do no lessons."

"Any lessons," Delphinia corrected. "The twins are still babies. You boys are old enough to know you must work for rewards. . .in this case, marbles. Tessie already understands that the true reward of a student is the knowledge you receive," she explained, although Tessie's look of boredom belied a real zeal for knowledge, or anything else at the moment.

"I did, however, find this tortoise-shell comb and, if you'd like, Tessie, I would be willing to consider it a little something extra, over and above the reward of knowledge."

Tessie eyed the comb trying to hide her excitement. It was the most beautiful hair piece she had ever seen and she desperately wanted it. As much as she wanted it, however, she would never concede that fact to Delphinia.

"I suppose it would make the boys try harder if they knew we were all working toward a reward," she responded.

Granny and Delphinia exchanged knowing smiles and the lessons began. The children worked hard on their studies and the days passed, some with more success than others. The boys finally were rewarded with all the marbles and Tessie had become the proud owner of the tortoise-shell comb.

When at last the snows abated and the roads were clear enough for school to resume the first week in December, both women heaved a sigh of relief, along with a prayer of thanksgiving. They waved from the doorway as the three older children climbed up on the buckboard and Jonathan drove off toward school, all of them agreeing the weather was still not fit to walk such a distance.

The children returned home that first day, each clutching a paper with their part for the Christmas pageant. Delphinia quickly realized the evenings would be spent with the children practicing elocution and memorization. Tessie was to portray Mary, but had detailed instructions that her red hair was to be completely tucked under a scarf.

"Why'd they pick her if they didn't want a redhead? It's not like she's the prettiest girl in class," Josh commented, tiring of the discussion of how to best cover Tessie's hair.

"They picked me because I'm the best actress in the school," Tessie retorted.

"I must be one of the smartest since the teacher picked me to be one of the Wise Men," Josh bantered back.

By this time, Joey was totally confused. "How come they picked me to be a shepherd, Granny?" he inquired. "Does that mean I have to take sheep with me to the school?"

Everyone broke into gales of laughter at his remark, as he stood there with a look of bewilderment on his face.

"No, sweet thing, you don't need any sheep," Granny replied. "But I think you all better get busy learning your lines instead of telling us how wise and talented you are."

After school the next day, Miss Sanders arrived to request that Nate or Nettie portray the Baby Jesus in the pageant. Just as Delphinia was beginning to explain that neither of them would hold still long enough for a stage production, both twins came toddling into the room. Squealing in delight and their hands smeared with jelly, they headed directly for the visitor. Delphinia was unable to head off the attack and Miss Sanders left soon after with jelly stains on the front of her dress and a withdrawal of her request for a Baby Jesus from the Wilshire home.

Granny, Jonathan, and Delphinia had been making plans for months, hoping the upcoming holiday would be a special time since this was the first Christmas the children, as well as Delphinia, would be without their parents.

"I want it to be a good Christmas, one we'll all remember fondly," Granny kept reminding them.

Jonathan made several trips to town for special purchases and while the children were at school, gifts were ordered through the mail or made by the women. Oranges, a rare treat for all of them, were poked full of cloves, and tins of dried apricots and candied fruits arrived. Gingerbread men were baked with the distinctive spice Granny ordered from back east and the children delighted in helping cut and bake them the Saturday before Christmas. Even Tessie seemed to enjoy the preparations, helping the younger children make decorations.

The day before Christmas Jonathan and the two older boys went in search of a tree with instructions from Granny that it not be too large. They came back with a somewhat scraggly cedar and placed it in the corner. The homemade garland and strings of popcorn were placed on the branches and Delphinia hung ornaments and a star that she had brought from home. The tin candle holders were clipped onto the tree, with a promise that the candles would be lit Christmas morning.

The day went by in a stir of confusion and soon everyone scurried to get ready for the Christmas pageant being held at the church. Jonathan worried the weather would be too hard on Granny, but she insisted on going. Dressed in her heaviest woolen dress and winter coat, Jonathan wrapped her frail figure in blankets, carried her to the wagon, and, placing her on a mattress stuffed with corn husks, tucked a twin on either side. Finally, he covered all of them with a feather comforter. The rest of the children piled in the back, all snuggling together to gain warmth from each other. Jonathan helped Delphinia to the seat beside him. Starting down the road, he pulled her closer with the admonition she would certainly be too cold sitting so far away. She did not resist, nor did she respond, but his touch caused her cheeks to feel fiery in the frosty night air.

The program was enchanting with each of the children performing admirably. The audience gave its enthusiastic approval and the evening ended with the group of delighted parents and relatives sharing cocoa and cookies. Miss Sanders proudly presented each of the children with a stick of peppermint candy as a gift for their hard work.

"I'm sorry I haven't been out to see you," George told Delphinia, offering her a cup of cocoa. "The weather has made it impossible, but I hope to come by again soon," he told her.

"We always look forward to your visits, George. I'm sorry I've missed you the last few times you've come to call," came Jonathan's reply from behind Delphinia. "You just come on out anytime. I'll make a point to be watching for you," he continued. "We're getting ready to leave, Phiney," he stated, holding out her coat and giving her a wink, sure that George would notice.

"Pastor Martin plans on coming out to visit soon," Delphinia informed Granny on the trip home.

"I think he's more interested in visiting Phiney than the rest of us, but I told him we'd be happy to have him anytime," Jonathan stated. "You two be sure and let me know when he comes calling so I don't miss another visit," he instructed and was disappointed when Delphinia did not give one of her quick retorts.

Once home, the children were soon tucked into bed, anxious for morning to arrive. Granny was quick to admit that she, too, needed her rest and apologetically requested that Delphinia complete the Christmas preparations. Before retiring, the older woman instructed Delphinia where everything had been hidden, fearful that a gift or two might be forgotten. Smiling and placing a kiss on her cheek, Delphinia reassured her that all would be ready by morning.

Christmas day was a joyous event of sparkling eyes and joyous laughter. The children were in good spirits, the tree was beautiful, and the gifts well received. Jonathan had gone hunting the morning before and returned with a wild turkey, which was the main attraction of the festive holiday meal. After dinner, Granny read the Christmas story from the Bible while the family sat in a circle around her listening intently, even the young twins. When she had finished, Jonathan began to sing "Silent Night" and the others joined in. One by one, they sang all the Christmas carols they could remember until Jonathan declared it was bedtime for the children. Not long after, Granny bid them good night, thanking them both for all they had done to make it such a wonderful day. "Don't stay up too long," she admonished, always in charge.

"We won't, Granny," answered Jonathan, smiling back at her.

As the burning candles flickered, Jonathan reached in his pocket, pulled out a small package, and handed it to Delphinia. Her face registered surprise.

"What's this for?" she inquired.

"It's a Christmas gift, from me to you. I didn't want to give it to you in front of the others."

"You shouldn't have, Jonathan," she chided as she slowly untied the ribbon and removed the wrapping to reveal a beautiful gold thimble on which the initials DEH had been engraved. Her face radiated as she examined it and placed it on her finger. "It's beautiful, Jonathan. I love it. How did you ever happen to choose a thimble?" she inquired.

"Granny told me about the quilt you and your mother stitched and how special it was to you. I figured sewing was important to you and I'd never seen you using a thimble when you were sewing. Granny said she didn't think you had one. The initials were Granny's idea."

"I'm surprised you didn't have it engraved P-E-H instead of D-E-H."

"To tell you the truth, I wanted to have it engraved with P-H-I-N-E-Y but Granny wouldn't hear of it and the engraver said it was too many letters for such a small piece," he laughed.

"I'd better be getting over to my place. It's getting late and Granny will have my hide if I'm not out of here soon," he said, rising from the his chair.

At the door he reached down and placed his hand alongside her face and lightly kissed her on the lips. "Merry Christmas, Phiney. I'll see you tomorrow," he said and headed toward his cabin.

Delphinia sat on the edge of her bed staring at the golden thimble and remembering Jonathan's kiss, still unsure she should trust any man again. *If I were to trust someone, George would probably be the safest choice,* she thought.

ten

Delphinia sat in the rocker, Nettie on one arm, Nathan on the other, watching their eyes slowly close in readiness for a nap. They had developed a real sense of independence, seldom wanting to be rocked anymore, except at bedtime. It was hard to believe that almost a year had passed since she left home. The birds were once again singing and the aroma of blooming honeysuckle gave notice of spring's arrival. New life had begun to appear in everything, except Granny. Her health fell in rapid decline throughout the winter and she lost the will to battle her debilitating illness any longer. It had been only a few weeks since her death, but life had taken a turn for the worse since her departure. Delphinia's sense of loss was extraordinary. Tessie had grown more sullen and less helpful, the boys seemed rowdier, the twins fussier, and Jonathan tried to cheer all of them, with sadness showing in his own eyes.

Delphinia thought of Granny's final words the morning she lay dying. "Remember I love you like a daughter, and the Lord loves you even more. Never turn from Him, Delphinia. I can see the peace you've gained since coming here and I don't want you to lose it. Nothing would make me sadder than to think my death would cause you to stumble in your faith.

"One more thing, my dear. Jonathan loves you and you love him. I'm not sure either of you realize it yet, but I'm sure God has wonderful plans for the two of you. You've learned well and there's nothing to fear. Jonathan will be close at hand whenever you need him," the dying woman had said as she reached up and wiped the tears from Delphinia's cheeks.

Shortly thereafter, she summoned Jonathan and, in hushed murmurs, they said their final goodbyes.

The services were held at the church and everyone in the surrounding area came to pay their tribute. Granny would have been pleased, not because they came to honor her, but because some of them hadn't been inside the church since it had been built!

Several days after the funeral, Pastor Martin came to visit and confided that the services had been planned by Granny. She had known it might be the only opportunity the minister would have to preach the plan of salvation to some of the homesteaders. Determined her death might provide eternal life for one of those settlers if they heard the message of God's love, she had ordered, "Don't talk about me, tell them about the precious Savior I've gone to join."

There had been no flowery eulogies, no words of praise about her many acts of charity, or sentimental stories about her life. Pastor Martin had given an eloquent sermon based on Romans 10:9-13 telling all those assembled that Granny's deepest desire had been consistent with that of her Lord. She wanted them to have the opportunity to receive Jesus Christ as their Savior. She wanted them to experience the joy of serving a Lord Who would be with them in the times of happiness as well as sorrow. She wanted them to know the pure joy and peace that could be attained in service to the living God. Yes, he pointed out, there would still be sorrow, even while faithfully serving the Lord. He told them there was no promise made that our lives would be free of unhappiness and grief but, he added, the Word of God does tell us we will not be alone at those times. We have comfort through our Lord, Jesus Christ.

"That is what Jesus wanted you to know, and that is what

Granny wanted you to know," he had said as he finished the message.

The service ended more like a revival meeting than a funeral. The pastor explained to those attending that if they had not received Jesus as their Savior, nothing would make Granny happier than to use this opportunity to take that step of commitment at her funeral. When two men and one young girl stepped forward, Delphinia was sure the angels in heaven were singing and that Granny was probably leading the chorus!

It had been a unique experience for all of them. The burial had taken place, followed by a baptism at the river and everyone had then returned to the church for dinner and visiting afterward.

Granny would have loved it!

The twins stirred in Delphinia's arms and carefully she placed them in bed, hoping they would not awaken. Hearing the sound of a horse coming toward the house, she walked to the porch and watched as George Martin approached, quickly returning his smile and wave. "It's good to see you, George," she welcomed as he climbed down from the horse. "Come in and I'll pour you some coffee."

"It's good to see you, too. Coffee sounds good. I hope you have some time so we can visit privately," he stated as they walked into the house.

"It appears you're in luck. The twins are napping, Tessie's gone to pick berries, and the older boys are with Jonathan," she answered.

"I really don't know how to begin," he stammered, taking a sip of coffee, "so I guess I'll just get to the heart of the matter."

"That's usually best," she encouraged, leaning forward.

"Delphinia, I don't know if you realize that I've come to care for you a great deal. We don't know each other well. . .I don't really think we could ever get to know each other very well as long as Jonathan's around. Anyway, I've been called to another church and must leave here by the end of the month. I'd like you to come with me. . .as my wife, of course," he stated.

"George. . .I don't know what to say. You've taken me by surprise," she said, her voice faltering. "You're a wonderful man but I don't think I could marry unless I was sure I loved you. I don't think a few weeks would assure us of that. Furthermore, I couldn't just leave the children. That's why I'm here, to care for them. I have an obligation to the bargain that was made, even if I wasn't a part of it," she stated, sadness evident in her voice.

"I'm not worried about the fact that you're not in love with me. I think our love for each other will grow once we're married. Your feeling of obligation to the Wilshires is admirable, and I certainly don't want to see the children left without someone to help, but I'm sure we can overcome that problem. That is, if you really want to," he said in a questioning manner.

"I'm not sure, George. I don't think I can give you an answer so quickly," she responded. *I'm just not ready to trust a man again,* she thought, *especially one I don't love.*

"Please don't think I'm placing pressure upon you, Delphinia, but I want to be absolutely honest. I've been calling on Katy McVay from time to time, also. I would prefer to marry you, but if you're going to turn me down, I need to know now," he replied.

"You mean if I reject you, you're going to ask Katy to marry you?"

"I am. I think highly of Katy, also. Unlike you, I believe love truly blossoms after marriage. You are my first choice, but I want to be married when I start my new assignment," he responded.

"Under the circumstances I hope she will accept your offer and the two of you will be very happy," Delphinia answered. Rising from her chair, she held out her hand to him. "I have truly enjoyed our friendship, George. I wish you much happiness and thank you for all the kindness you've extended. I am honored you would ask me to marry you but I think we both now realize our thoughts on love and marriage differ enough that your choice should be someone else."

"I'm sorry we can't make this work," he replied as they walked outside and he got on his horse.

"Good luck with Katy," she called out, watching him ride down the path. Slowly she walked into the house and sat down in the rocker, contemplating the consequences of her decision, wondering if she should change her mind and go after him.

Voices from outside brought her back to the present and the twins began to stir in the bedroom. Jonathan, Josh, and Joey came rushing into the room, concern and excitement evident as they all tried to talk at once.

"I need your help, Phiney. The boys can watch the twins," Jonathan shouted above the boys' chatter.

"Let's find Tessie. I'd rather have her stay with them. What's going on?" she asked, not yet convinced it was necessary to leave the twins in the care of their over-anxious brothers.

"She's gone to pick berries. I need you now. The cow's giving birth and she's having a hard time. Come on," he shouted, rushing to the barn to grab some rope and then running for the pasture.

Soon after Delphinia left the cabin, she could hear the cow's deep bellowing and she wondered what Jonathan could possibly expect her to do. She did not know anything about birthing children, let alone animals, and besides, couldn't a cow do that without help? she wondered.

Nellie, the small black heifer was lying down as Josie, the older brown and white cow, appeared to stand guard a short distance away. Jonathan was already at Nellie's side, motioning Delphinia to hurry. Not sure what to expect, her gait had grown slower and slower as she approached the laboring animal. Nothing could have prepared her for the experience. The cow's eyes were open wide, registering fear and pain. A low, bellowing moan came from deep in the animal's throat just as Delphinia walked up beside Jonathan.

"I don't know what to do. I think we should have Josh ride for Mr. Aplington. He'll be able to help," she offered, near panic.

"There's no time for that. If we don't get this calf out, we'll lose both of them. I don't want to lose the calf, but it's probably already dead. I'll hold onto Nellie while you reach up inside her and see if you can grab hold of the calf's legs. If you can, pull with all your might."

"I can't do that! You want *me* to reach up inside the cow? That is the most absurd thing I've ever heard. . .not to mention how offensive. If it's so important, do it yourself," she retorted, her face registering disgust.

"*Delphinia,* this cow is going to die! I don't have time to listen to your nonsense. You can't hold onto Nellie. Now reach in there and pull!" he commanded as froth oozed from Nellie's mouth and her tongue lolled to the side.

Going down on her knees, Delphinia closed her eyes and felt her hands begin to shake. "All right, I can do this," she told herself, peeking out of one eye. Taking in a gulp of air, she thrust her arm high inside the cow. The assault was met by Nellie's bellow and a flailing leg. "I thought you were going to hold her!" Delphinia screamed.

"I'm trying. Can you feel anything?"

"I think so. . .yes. Jonathan, hold her still! How do you

expect me to take care of this when you're not doing your part?"

He looked at her in astonishment. *"You're taking care of it?"*

"I don't see you doing much of anything," she grunted, leaning back and pulling with all her might. "This isn't working. I think it moved a little but I can't get a good hold."

Jonathan grabbed the piece of rope he had brought from the barn and tossed it to her. "Reach in and tie that around it's legs. Be sure you get both legs."

"This isn't a quilting party, Jonathan," she rebutted. "Next you'll be telling me to embroider a lazy-daisy stitch on its rump."

Her remark brought the hint of a smile to his face. "Make a loop in the rope, slide it around the legs, and tighten it. When you're sure the rope is tight, try pulling again. Once you feel it coming, don't let up. If you slack off, it might get hip-locked and we'll lose both of them," he instructed.

All of a sudden, the heat was stifling and Delphinia felt herself begin to retch. "Not now, Phiney. There isn't time for you to be sick," he commanded.

"I'll try to keep that in mind," she replied curtly, tying a slipknot into the rope.

"You need to hurry!" he yelled.

"Jonathan, you are not helping this predicament with your obtrusive behavior! How do you expect the cow to remain calm if you keep hollering all the time," she preached at him. "I have the rope ready, and if you will kindly hold Nellie still this time, I will begin. Everything is going to be fine."

His jaw went slack as she finished her short speech. Where had that come from? She seemed totally in command and a calmness had taken the place of the near hysteria she had exhibited only minutes before. He kept his eyes on her and tightly gripped the heifer when she nodded she was ready to begin.

With almost expert ease, and over the vigorous protests of Nellie, she managed to secure both of the calf's front legs. Being careful not to let up, she worked arduously, pulling and tugging, her arms aching as the calf was finally pulled into the world. The calf's feeble bawl affirmed its birth. "It's alive," she said, tears streaming down her face.

"Let's hope it stays that way, and let's hope·Nellie does the same," Jonathan answered.

"They're both going to be fine," she replied confidently.

"Take your apron and clean out it's nose, while I check Nellie," he ordered.

"Yes, sir! Any other commands?" she inquired, watching the new mother turn and begin lapping her tongue over the calf in a slow, deliberate manner.

"Not right now. It looks like Nellie's going to be a good mama. She's got her a nice lookin' little calf," he said, ignoring the barb she had given.

Delphinia sat back on her heels watching the two animals in wonderment. "There surely was a transformation in your attitude when you were helping me," Jonathan commented. "At first I thought you were going to be less help than Josh. One minute you were retching and the next you were ordering me around and taking charge," he laughed.

Turning to look at him, she quietly replied, "It was God Who took charge, Jonathan. I merely prayed. But I knew that as soon as I finished that prayer for help, everything was going to be all right."

"You're quite a mystery, Phiney," he said, slowly shaking his head. "First, you're giving me the devil and next, you're praising God."

"I'm not sure I'm such a mystery. I criticize you only when it's needed," she laughed. "I do know I fail to praise God enough for all He does. I sometimes forget we serve a mighty God and that much can be wrought through prayer. My mother taught me that when I was very young, and I watched Granny live it daily." She reached up from where she sat and grasped his extended hand.

"Thanks for your help, Phiney. I couldn't have done it without you. I'm sure if Nellie and her baby could thank you, they would." Almost as if on cue, the tiny calf let out a warbling cry, causing both of them to smile.

"By the way, was that George Martin I saw leaving a while ago?" he questioned later, as they walked toward the house.

"Yes. He's been called to another church and will be leaving the end of the month," she answered.

"George is a fine preacher, but I can't say I'm sorry to see him leave," he responded.

"You may be. He's gone to ask for Katy McVay's hand in marriage," she told him, sure that that would take the smug grin from his face.

"Katy? Why would he be asking for Katy's hand. I know he's fond of you."

"He asked for my hand," she answered, saying nothing further.

"He what?" Jonathan pulled her to an abrupt stop. "What did you tell him?"

"I told him, no."

"So now he's gone to ask Katy?"

"It appears so," she answered and then related enough of their conversation to hopefully stop his questions, while watching his face for reaction.

"I didn't know she had taken a shine to the preacher. They might make a good match," he replied. "The less competition the better, as far as I'm concerned," he mumbled under his breath.

"What did you say?" she asked, turning toward him.

"Nothing to concern yourself with," he replied and began whistling as they walked to the house.

eleven

With the coming of early summer, the days grew longer and the beauty of nature began to unfold. The twins were able to play outside as Delphinia, aided by Jonathan, prepared the ground for her garden. Surprisingly, she found herself anxious to begin the arduous task, wondering if she would remember all that Granny had taught her. She felt challenged to prove she had been a capable student, worthy of the older woman's confidence.

Jonathan assured her she would be an adept gardener, pointing to the fact that she had nagged him almost continuously until he had given in and tilled enough ground for an early planting of potatoes in late March. Besides, the strawberries were already beginning to blossom, thanks to her attentive care and the cooperative weather.

Nate and Nettie found enjoyment following behind and playing in the turned soil, occasionally spotting a worm or some other crawling creature that they would attempt to capture. In late afternoon, the older children would return from school and go about their chores, enjoying the freedom that the change of season allowed. All, but Tessie. If she found enjoyment in anything, she hid it from Delphinia.

It seemed that no matter how earnestly Delphinia prayed, she had not been able to make an inroad with Tessie. She tried everything from cajoling to ignoring her but nothing seemed to work. The young girl was determined to do all in her power to make those around her miserable, particularly Delphinia. She was not unkind to the other children, yet she did not go out of her way to help them. She performed her chores but if Delphinia requested additional help, she would become angry or sulk. When Jonathan was about, she was on her best behavior although it was obvious that even at those times, she was unhappy.

Saturday arrived bright and sunny and Jonathan declared it would be a wonderful day for fishing down at the creek. In return for preparation of a picnic lunch, he offered to take all of the children on the excursion and give Delphinia some much-needed time alone. She was overwhelmed by the offer and questioned whether he thought the twins would allow him to do any fishing. When he assured her he would be able to handle the twins, he began packing a lunch for their outing.

"I'm not going," Tessie announced in a voice that almost defied either of them to oppose her decision.

"I'd like you to come with us, Tessie," her uncle answered, sitting down at the kitchen table with a cup of coffee. "Delphinia has little time to herself. She's had to care for all of us without much opportunity for leisure. I hope you'll reconsider your decision."

"If she doesn't want me around, I'll stay out on the porch or in the orchard," she petulantly answered.

"No, I'd like to have you stay with me, Tessie. If you don't want to go fishing, we can enjoy the day together," Delphinia replied sweetly, looking over at Jonathan to let him know she would not mind.

The children were so excited that Delphinia finally sent them outdoors until she completed packing the lunch and Jonathan was prepared to leave. Following him to the porch, Delphinia noticed the questioning look in his eyes as he turned to bid her farewell.

"We'll be just fine," she assured him. "It's you who will be in for a day of it, believe me! I'm sure there will be no fish returning with you, so I'll have some beans and corn bread ready," she bantered.

"We'll see about that!" Jonathan responded, accepting her challenge. Lifting Nettie upon his shoulders, he grabbed Nate's chubby hand and cautioned Josh not to forget their lunch. Joey ran along carrying the fishing poles Jonathan had crafted, all of them full of eagerness to catch a fish for supper. Waving after the departing group, Delphinia wished them good luck and stood watching until they were out of sight.

Slowly returning to the kitchen, she began clearing the breakfast dishes from the table. "I think I'll make gooseberry pies for dessert tonight, Tessie. If you'll wash off the berries while I finish up the dishes, we can be done in no time. I thought I'd go out to the barn and go through my trunks. I have some things stored out there I'd like to use."

Although there was no response, Tessie picked up the pail of berries and headed toward the well to fetch water. Delphinia noticed that instead of returning to the kitchen to visit, she sat isolated on the porch until her task was completed, and then reappeared.

As Delphinia mixed the pie dough and began to roll it, she asked if Tessie would like to accompany her to the barn.

"I suppose. There's nothing else to do," came the girl's curt reply. Nothing further passed between them and once the gooseberries had been sweetened and poured into the pie shells, Delphinia placed them in the oven.

"I think these will be fine while we're down at the barn. You remind me they're in the oven, if I get forgetful. Once I get going through those trunks, I may get absent-minded," she smiled, removing her apron and throwing it over the back of a wooden chair.

Tessie followed her, giving no acknowledgment that any words had been spoken.

The barn was warm and the smell of hay wafted through the air as Delphinia proceeded to the far stall to see the calf she had pulled into the world only a few weeks ago. How he was growing! Josh had named him "Lucky" and they had agreed it was a good choice.

Tessie stood by waiting, a look of boredom evident on her face, but Delphinia pretended not to notice. They made their way toward the rear of the barn and, after brushing off the dirt, unlatched the hasp and opened the trunk. Lifting the items out one by one, Delphinia began sorting into piles those belongings she wished to take into the house and the ones she would leave packed. From time to time, Tessie would show a spark of interest in an item, but would not allow herself to inquire. Near the bottom of the trunk, wrapped in a woolen blanket, Delphinia found her mother's china teapot. She carefully unwrapped it and stared at it as if she expected it to come to life.

"We've already got a teapot," Tessie exclaimed, wanting her to hurry up.

"Yes, I know. But this was my mother's teapot and her mother's before her. It is very special to me. In fact, I remember the last time it was used," she continued, not particularly caring if the girl listened. She needed to recall the memory, just to validate who she had been, even if no one else cared.

"You may remember I told you about the quilt that's on my bed. My mother and I spent many hours making that quilt. It's probably my most precious possession. When I had finally completed the final stitches and it had passed Mama's inspection, we had a celebration. My mother seldom used this china teapot. It sat on a shelf in the cabinet because she feared it might get broken. It was one of the few possessions her mother had passed on to her when she married and moved to Illinois," Delphinia related as Tessie stared toward the barn door.

"Anyway, that day my mother had baked bread and she said we were going to have a tea party to commemorate the completion of my first quilt. She brewed a special mint tea in this teapot and cut slices of warm bread for us. She even opened one of her jars of preserves and we had such a gay time," she reminisced.

"Do you think the pies are done yet?" was Tessie's only remark to the account Delphinia had just given.

"What? Oh, yes, I suppose they'll soon be ready," answered Delphinia, coming back to the present. Lovingly she wrapped the teapot back in the woolen blanket and placed it in the trunk, knowing this was not the time to move it into the cabin. *Perhaps, one day it will sit on a shelf in my home,* she hoped.

Swiftly, she placed one pile of her belongings back in the trunk and bundled the rest in a tablecloth. Walking back to the house with her collection, she could smell the pies and quickened her step.

"Tessie, check those pies while I put this in my room, please," she requested as she stepped into her bedroom, coming face to face with a large Indian bouncing on the edge of her bed.

Stifling the scream that was caught in her throat, she attempted to smile and remain calm. "Tessie, there's an Indian sitting on my bed," she said, staring directly at the warrior. "Try and quietly leave the cabin. I'm hopeful he thinks I'm talking to him, so don't say anything, just leave. He doesn't look like the other Indians that have been to the house. Go to the Aplingtons' for help."

The Indian continued to bounce on the mattress until she quit speaking and then, with alarming speed, he jumped up, pushed his way by her, and ran into the kitchen. Delphinia turned to see him holding Tessie by the arm, pulling her back inside the house. He slammed the door shut and, standing in front of the barrier, motioned they should not attempt to leave.

Slowly he walked toward Tessie and began circling her,

occasionally stopping and staring. Tears began to trickle down the girl's face and Delphinia moved closer to place an arm around her, only to have it slapped away by the intruder.

"Stay," he commanded Delphinia, pointing to the spot where she was standing. He moved closer to Tessie and grabbed a handful of her hair and grunted. He stood trans-fixed, rubbing the locks of red hair back and forth between his fingers, occasionally making some sound.

Tessie, overcome by fear and sure he was planning to scalp her, could stand it no longer and lunged toward Delphinia for protection.

"You, sit," he commanded, pushing the young girl into a chair.

"Obviously, he understands some English, Tessie. Just try to remain calm and I'll see if we can communicate," Delphinia said as soothingly as possible.

Issuing a prayer for help, Delphinia smiled at the uninvited visitor and, while making hand motions, asked, "You, hungry? Want to eat?"

She walked toward one of the pies cooling on the table and lifted it toward him as an offering. Lowering and raising his head in affirmation, he reached across the table and, forming his hand into a scoop, dug into the pie and brought out a handful of steaming gooseberries. Letting out a howl, he flung his arm, causing the berries to fly in all directions about the room. Tessie was close to hysteria, unable to control her high-pitch laughter, which further angered the injured warrior.

Dear God, Delphinia prayed silently, *I'm relying on Mark 11:24. You promise that if we believe we've already received what we're praying for, it will be ours. Well, Lord, I believe this Indian is going to leave our house and not harm either of us. The problem is, I'm afraid things have gotten out of control, what with his burned hand and Tessie's continual outbursts. So I'd be real thankful if I could claim that promise right now.*

Assured the matter was safely in God's hands and would be favorably resolved, Delphinia confidently offered the glowering trespasser a wet towel for his hand. He grunted and wrapped the moist cloth around the burn. Tessie became silent until the Indian once again walked to where she sat and began caressing her hair.

"Please, Tessie, try to remain composed. The Lord is going to see us through this, but you must act rationally. I'm going to try and find out what he wants," Delphinia quietly advised. The blue eyes that looked back at her were apprehensive, but Tessie did not cry.

Considering the pie disaster, Delphinia thought it best she try to distract the Indian with something other than food. Eyeing a small mirror, she tentatively offered it. Although somewhat suspicious, curiosity won out and he took the object from her hand. At first, his reflection startled him but then, as he made faces at himself in the glass, he seemed pleased. Soon, he was walking around the room holding it up to objects and peeking to see what had been reproduced for him. Standing behind Tessie, he held the mirror in front of her, producing an image of both their faces that, from the sounds he was making, he found highly amusing.

While the Indian continued his antics with the mirror, Delphinia tried to assemble her thoughts. It was obvious he was quite fascinated with Tessie's red hair. If only she knew what he was planning. No sooner had that thought rushed through her head than the Indian grabbed Tessie's arm and started toward the door.

"We go," he pronounced in a commanding voice.

Once again Tessie broke into wails and Delphinia's heart began pounding as she screamed, "No, stop!" and motioned him into her bedroom. Dragging Tessie along, he followed and was met by Delphinia's display of belongings she had just carried from the barn.

"Take these things," she said, pointing to the array on her bed. "She stays here," she continued, trying to pull Tessie beside her.

A deep grunt emitted while he sorted through the items. He was smiling, which pleased Delphinia, and she whispered to Tessie she should move behind her. He did not seem to notice the movement, or so they thought, as he pulled the tablecloth around the items and tied a large knot.

"I take," he said, placing the bundle on the floor and pointing to himself. "Her, too," he said, indicating Tessie.

Well, this is really beginning to try my patience, Delphinia thought. *Not only is he going to take all my treasures, but he wants Tessie, to boot. I just won't tolerate that kind of behavior. After all, fair is fair!*

Moving a step toward him and placing both hands on her hips, Delphinia looked him full in the eyes and vehemently retorted, "No. Not her." She shook her head negatively and pointed to Tessie. "She's mine," and placed an arm around the girl to indicate possession.

Somewhat taken aback by Delphinia's aggressive behavior, the Indian stood observing the two young women. Raising an arm to his head and lifting a bit of hair, he pointed toward Tessie.

"Oh, no! He wants to scalp me!" the child screamed.

"I don't think he's ever seen red hair before, Tessie. Perhaps if we would just cut a lock or two and give it to him. What do you think?" asked Delphinia, not sure of what the Indian wanted.

Tessie merely nodded her head and Delphinia walked to her bureau, removed her sewing scissors, and walked toward Tessie, all under the close observation of the man. Reaching toward the mass of red ringlets, Delphinia snipped a thick lock of hair and handed it to the warrior. He smiled and seemed in agreement.

"You, go now," Delphinia ordered.

Stooping to pick up the bundle, he reached across the bed and in one sweeping motion pulled the quilt from Delphinia's bed and wrapped it around himself.

"Oh, no you don't," yelled Delphinia. "Not my quilt. That's mine and you can't have it," she screamed, attempting to pull it from his shoulders.

Angered by her actions, the Indian threw down the quilt and reached to grab Tessie.

Realizing she had provoked him and was about to lose her advantage, she tried to calm herself. "No, not her. Take me," she said, throwing herself in front of the girl.

The intruder backed up slightly and Delphinia, with tears in her eyes, pleaded, "You can have my quilt, you can have me and all of my belongings. Just don't take this child. She needs to be here with her family. I'll go with you willingly, and I'll give you anything from this house you want. . .just not the girl. Please, not her," she begged.

She did not know how much he understood, or what he would do, but she lifted the quilt back around his shoulders and then held out the bundle that had been resting on the floor. Looking directly in her eyes, he took the bundle and, wearing her quilt across his shoulders, slowly walked from the room and out of the house.

twelve

Hearing the door close, Delphinia rushed into the kitchen and lowered the wooden bar they used as a lock. Returning to the bedroom, she found Tessie huddled in the far corner of the bedroom, legs drawn to her chest and with her head buried low, resting on her knees. Going to her, Delphinia enveloped the child with both her arms and began talking to her in a soothing, melodic voice. Tessie did not respond and Delphinia began to worry that she had slipped away into the recesses of her own mind, like those people she had heard about, who were sent off to insane asylums.

"Tessie," she said quietly, "this isn't going to do at all. The Lord has kept His promise and we're safe from harm. Now you're going to have to do your part." Moving back slightly and cupping her hands under the girl's chin, she lifted the beautiful crown of red hair until Tessie was eye to eye with her.

Her eyes are vacant and she's not going to respond, Delphinia thought.

"Tessie, I know you may not hear me, but in case you do, I apologize," and then Delphinia landed a resounding slap across the girl's cheek.

"What are you doing?" Tessie asked, dismayed by the act.

Overjoyed with the results, Delphinia hugged her close, laughing and crying simultaneously. "Oh, Tessie, I was so worried you weren't going to respond. I tried to arouse you, but to no avail. I'm so sorry, but I didn't know what else to do but give you a good whack."

"Are you sure he's gone?" the girl sobbed, tightly embracing Delphinia.

"Yes, he's gone, and everything is fine," she reassured, returning the embrace.

Tessie's body trembled and once again she broke into racking sobs. "Why did he try to take me? What if he comes back? What are we going to do?" she wailed between sobs and gulps of breath, her body heaving in distress.

"Tessie, calm yourself. Everything is fine. He won't come back. He's probably miles away by now," she crooned, wiping the girl's tears.

"But what if he isn't? What if he's outside lurking about, just waiting for one of us?" she questioned, faltering in her attempt to gain composure.

"If he wanted one of us, he wouldn't have left the cabin," Delphinia answered, holding the girl and stroking her hair. "We're fine, Tessie, just fine," she assured for what seemed like the hundredth time.

Slowly Tessie's body began to relax and finally she gave Delphinia a half-hearted smile. "Perhaps we should go sit in the kitchen where it's a bit more comfortable," she suggested.

"That's a wonderful idea," Delphinia responded, her cramped body needing to stretch. "I'll put the kettle on for tea."

"We need to talk," Tessie whispered.

"I'd like that very much," came Delphinia's response.

Making their way into the kitchen, Tessie wearily dropped onto one of the wooden chairs. "I know I've been spiteful to you for no apparent reason. You didn't do anything but try to be nice to me. I've treated you horribly and in return you offered yourself to that savage. You allowed him to take your beautiful quilt and other belongings. I know that quilt was very special and yet you gave it willingly for me. Why did you do it?" she coaxed, tears slipping down her face.

Delphinia poured two cups of steaming tea and sat down beside her. "When I first came here I anticipated you would resent me. Your Uncle Jonathan had forewarned me you had not accepted the deaths of your parents. I must add, however, that I didn't expect your bitterness to last this long! Granny and I prayed for you every day, Tessie, and I have continued since her death. We both realized you were in torment and, although it has been difficult at times, I have tried to remember your pain when you've treated me impertinently," she smiled, pausing to take a sip of tea.

"Yes, but *why* did you do it?" she implored.

"This is going to take a few minutes of explanation, Tessie. Please try to be patient. I've been waiting for a very long time for this moment to arrive."

Tessie smiled and Delphinia continued. "You're right about the quilt. It was my pride and joy. But it is merely an object, not a living, breathing child of God, like you. In my prayers, I have consistently asked God to show me a way to give you peace from your anger and turmoil. That Indian's appearance while we were here alone was God's answer to my prayers. Had I not offered myself and those possessions that were important to me, you might never have believed that anybody loved you. I'm sure you know the verse in the Bible that says, 'Greater love hath no man than this,—' "

" 'That a man lay down his life for his friends.' John 15:13," interrupted Tessie. "Granny taught me that verse long ago."

"I love you that much, Tessie, and Jesus loves you that much, too. He sacrificed His life for you, so that you could live. . .not be consumed by hate and anger," she said, watching the play of emotions that crossed the girl's face.

"I'm not just angry because Ma and Pa died, Phiney," she began. "Nobody knows everything that happened that day, except me."

"Perhaps you'd feel better if you confided in someone. I know Jonathan would sympathize with anything you told him," Delphinia encouraged.

"No, I think perhaps I should tell you. Uncle Jonathan might not be so understanding. You see, it's my fault. I killed my parents. *Do you still love me now?*" she asked, her voice trembling.

"Yes, Tessie, I still love you. But since you've taken me into your confidence, would you consider telling me what part you played in their deaths?" she asked in a kindly manner.

Her eyes seemed to glaze over as she recounted the events of that day. Delphinia noted the story was almost identical to what Jonathan had previously related to her on the wagon train. "So now you can see how I am the cause of their deaths," she said, ending the narrative.

Delphinia stared at her, dumbfounded. "No, Tessie, I don't. Jonathan related that exact account to me before my arrival. Please explain what was your fault," she queried.

"Don't you see? I was the one who wanted to go the creek bed route. If we had gone the other way, we would have been safe," she wailed.

"Oh, Tessie," Delphinia whispered, embracing the child, "there is no way we can possibly guess what would have happened if you'd taken the other route. Perhaps the wagon would have been struck by lightning, causing it to go up in flames. Perhaps one of the horses would have broken a leg in a chuckhole causing the wagon to overturn and crush all of you. Any number of things could have happened. We'll never know. What we do know is that the lives of you children were saved. You're not guilty of anything. You asked your father to travel a different road. He knew the dangers that route held and he made a decision to go that direction. His choice was based on knowledge he had available to him.

It didn't appear it was going to rain and there were no more hazards than the other road might have had in store for his family. You have no fault in their deaths and no reason to condemn yourself. Somehow, you must accept that fact. Don't die with your parents, Tessie. Let them live through you. If you'll only allow it, others will see the love and gentleness of Sarah and Jake Wilshire shining in your eyes. That's what they would have wanted and I think if you'll search your heart, you know that already."

"I know you're right, but it hurts so much and I don't want them to be forgotten," she confided.

Clasping her hands around Tessie's, Delphinia looked at her with a sense of understanding and said, "How could they ever be forgotten with five such wonderful children? You're a testimony to their lives. It's not easy to lose your parents, but God will help fill that emptiness, if you'll allow it. It's up to you, but I don't think you want a life full of unhappiness and brooding any more than I do. Pray for peace and joy, Tessie, and it will come to you when you least expect it."

The girl gave a half-hearted smile through her tears and whispered, "I'll try."

"I know you will and I'll be praying right along with you."

❧

Jonathan had never been so exhausted. *I don't know how Phiney keeps up with these children all day long, day after day,* he thought.

He lost count of the times he had chased after the twins, both of them determined to wander off and pick a flower or run after a squirrel. When they weren't trying to explore, they were playing at the edge of the water, caking mud in their hair and all over their clothes. With no soap or washcloth available, he decided the only way to get them presentable was to dunk them in the creek before starting home. Josh and Joey thought it was hilarious watching their Uncle

Jonathan put a twin under each arm and wade into the cool water. Their squeals of protest only added to the boys' enjoyment of the event.

"You guys quit your laughin' and get our gear picked up. It's time we headed back to the house. They'll be expecting some fish for supper, so get a move on."

The air was warm as they made their way through the orchard and, as they approached the cabin, the boys were still chattering about who caught the biggest fish and who tangled the fishing lines. On and on it went, Jonathan ignoring them for the most part and hoping the twins were "dried out" before Phiney got hold of them.

"Wonder why they got the door closed, Uncle Jonathan. You suppose they went visiting somewhere and you'll have to cook the fish?" Josh questioned.

"I don't know, Josh. But if they're gone, you can forget the fish. I'm not cooking. I've about had all the women's work I can stand for one day."

"Ahhh, Uncle Jon, please," came from both boys in unison.

"Let's just wait and see if they're home. Run ahead and check the door, Josh."

"I can't get in, Uncle Jon. It's locked," he yelled back to them.

Terror ran through Jonathan. Why would Phiney have the door barred? There had been no rumors of problems with the Indians and it did not appear that anyone else was at the cabin. Placing the twins on the ground, he took off at full speed toward the cabin, calling back to Joey to remain with the smaller children until he was sure all was safe.

"Phiney, Phiney!" he yelled as he reached the entry and began pounding on the door.

"I'm coming, Jonathan. You needn't yell," she answered, allowing him entry.

His eyes immediately fixed on Tessie. Bedraggled, a red hand print across her cheek, her face wet from tears, and her eyes puffy from crying, he went racing to her, swooping her into his arms.

"What's happened here?" he asked in an accusatory tone, looking directly at Delphinia.

She could feel the hair on the back of her neck begin to bristle at his tone. "Why I've just finished beating her, Jonathan. Why do you ask?" she quietly responded with an angelic smile.

Both women began to laugh, causing Tessie to erupt into loud hiccups. Jonathan stared at the two of them as if they had gone mad. "If you'll quit acting so preposterous, we'll explain what happened. Where are the twins?" Delphinia inquired. "I hope you haven't forgotten them," she smirked.

"That's enough," he answered, calming somewhat. "Joey, you can bring the twins up now," he called out the door.

"Josh, go help him and bring the fish. I'm sure Phiney is ready to eat crow while we eat fish," he said, tilting his head to one side and giving her a crooked grin.

As Josh came in, carrying a string of fish and pulling Nettie along under protest, Jonathan said, "I'd be happy to sit here and listen to the events of the afternoon, ladies, while you fry that fish."

But he was not prepared for the story he heard and continually interrupted them, pacing back and forth while they related the tale. Tessie completed the narrative by telling how the Indian finally left the cabin with Delphinia's possessions and her quilt wrapped around him.

"There's an even more important part, but I'll tell you that when we're alone, Uncle Jon," Tessie remarked.

Delphinia smiled and nodded toward the door. "Why don't the two of you take a short walk while I finish supper. We'll be fine in here."

When they returned, Jonathan immediately went to Delphinia and, placing his arms around her, whispered, "How can I ever thank you? She's finally come back to us."

"It wasn't me that did it, Jonathan. It was answered prayer," she responded. "However, if you're determined to find a way to thank me, you can fry this fish for supper," she said, laughing at the look of disdain he displayed with that request.

Grinning, he released her and said, "I should have known you'd be quick with an answer."

thirteen

The morning dawned glorious with puffy white clouds that appeared to almost touch the earth. A pale orange sun shone through, causing a profusion of magnificent colors and the promise of a gorgeous day. Looking out the front door of the place she now called home, Delphinia wondered how anything could be more beautiful. The view nearly took her breath away.

She waved her arm in welcome to Jonathan who was coming from the barn, apparently already through with some of his morning chores. "Breakfast is just about ready. Isn't it a splendid morning?" she called out.

"That it is. We couldn't have planned a better day for going to town," he responded.

Delphinia watched as he continued toward her, knowing Granny had been right. She did love this giant of a man who had turned her world upside down. Her day became joyful just watching him walk into a room. Her feelings were undeniably true and they had been for quite some time, although she did not want to admit it. She had given this thing called "love" a considerable amount of thought. Late at night lying in bed, she had gone through the diverse emotions she had felt for Jonathan since that first day when they had met back in Illinois. They seemed to range from dread and dislike to admiration and caring. For some time she had had difficulty keeping herself from staring at him all the time. Even Tessie had mentioned it and knowingly grinned.When she considered how Jonathan might feel toward her, she was not so sure her feelings were fully returned. He treated her well, was kind and considerate, and listened to her before making decisions. But that was not love. Also, he treated everyone that way. He had kissed her on a few occasions but it seemed that each of those times had either ended in a quarrel or could be interpreted as pity. She realized he had tried to make the preacher jealous with his attention but she was sure that was so he would not have to go looking for someone else to care for the children. On several occasions, he had mentioned he could not get along without her, but she reasoned that that was because he needed help with the children, not because of love.

"Are those the biscuits I smell burning?" Jonathan asked, bringing her back to the present. "That's just about once a day now you're scorching something, isn't it?" He sat down at the table with a cup of freshly poured coffee. "Is there something wrong with the stove or have you just forgotten how to cook these days?" he joked.

"I think she's in love," Tessie teased.

"That will be enough out of you, Tessie. Get busy and dress the twins so we can get started for town," Delphinia responded angrily, knowing the girl had spoken the truth.

"She's only having fun, Phiney. You don't need to bite her head off," Jonathan responded, giving Tessie a quick hug and nodding for her to get the twins ready.

Irritated with herself for scolding the girl, Delphinia walked into the other room and sat down on the bed. "I'm sorry, Tessie. My remark was uncalled for. Perhaps it made me uncomfortable."

"Why, because it's the truth? Anyone can see you're in love with Uncle Jon. You look like a lovesick calf when he comes into a room, so it's hard not to notice." They both burst out laughing at her remark and Jonathan, hearing the giggles from the bedroom, smiled in relief, pleased that this had not caused discord between the two now that they had become friends.

"How 'bout we get this burned breakfast eaten and get started toward town before nightfall, unless you two would rather stay here and do chores all day," Jonathan called from the kitchen.

That statement brought everyone clamoring for the table and they all agreed the biscuits weren't too bad if you put lots of gravy on them. Delphinia good-naturedly took their bantering and soon they were loaded into the wagon and on their way. Tessie offered to sit in back with both of the twins, allowing Jonathan and Delphinia a small amount of privacy.

"How many supplies do you plan on buying today?" Jonathan queried.

"Just the usual, except Tessie and I want to spend a little time looking about for some thread and fabric. In fact, if you could keep an eye on the younger ones while we do that, I'd be thankful," she responded.

"What are the two of you planning now?" he asked with a grin.

"Tessie's asked me to help her finish the quilt that Sarah started before her death. She wants to use it for her bed. We decided to purchase the items needed to finish it today and, as soon as harvest is over, we'll get started with our sewing."

"You hadn't told me about that. I can't tell you how pleased it makes me that Tessie has finally accepted your friendship. I know Sarah and Granny would be mighty happy," he smiled.

"I think they would be, too, Jonathan. She's a sweet girl and I hope completing the quilt with her will be good for both of us. Somehow, quilting with my mother gave me a feeling of closeness. We would visit and laugh together as we sewed the stitches, knowing each one helped hold the quilt together and made it more beautiful. It's much like the threads of love that tie folks' hearts together. There are the small, tightly sewn stitches, close together, like a family. Then there are the larger, scattered stitches, like the friends we make in our lifetime. I believe God weaves all those threads together in a beautiful pattern to join our hearts and make us who we are, don't you think?"

He looked down at her and a slow smile crossed his face. "You, know, you never cease to amaze me with your ideas. That's a beautiful thought, and I agree," he answered, placing his hand on top of Delphinia's.

She glanced toward him and he was staring down at their two hands. She watched as he enveloped hers and gave a gentle squeeze. Slowly, he looked up and met her watchful eyes as Delphinia felt her cheeks flush and a quiver of emotions run through her entire being. The question in her eyes was evident.

"Yes," he said, looking deep into the two, dark brown liquid pools.

"Yes, what?" she inquired. "I didn't ask you anything."

"Yes, you did, Phiney, and the answer is, yes, I love you very much."

Leaning over toward him, she said, "I can't hear you above the children's singing."

"I said I love you, Delphinia Elizabeth Hughes," he said and leaned down to gently place a kiss on her lips.

The children burst forth with hoots of laughter and loud clapping at the scene unfolding in front of them. Jonathan joined in their laughter and then lifted Delphinia's hand to his lips for a kiss, just as they arrived at the general store.

"Jonathan, there's some mail over here for ya'," called Mr. McVay from the rear of the store. "Think there's one in there for Phiney, too."

"For me?" she questioned, looking at Jonathan. "Who would be writing me?"

"Only one way to find out. Let's take a look," he answered as they headed toward the voice.

Jonathan quickly perused the mail and handed over the envelope bearing Delphinia's name. He could see from the return address that it was from her father.

"It's from my pa," she commented. "From the looks of the envelope, he's in Colorado. I think I'll wait until I get home to read it," she said, folding the letter in half and placing it in her skirt pocket.

"I'll go give my order to Mrs. McVay and as soon as she's finished, Tessie and I can look at fabric. I better get back to the children. It looks like the twins are going to try and get into the cracker barrel head first," she exclaimed, moving toward the front of the store at a quick pace.

Jonathan smiled after her but could not shake the feeling of foreboding that had come over him ever since he had seen the letter.

Why now? he thought. *What does he want after all this time?* He did not know how long he had been wandering through the store, aimlessly looking at a variety of tools and dry goods when Tessie's voice brought him to attention.

"Uncle Jon, come on, we've got the order filled except for the thread and fabric. It's your turn to look after the twins."

"Sure, be right there. You women go pick out your sewing things," he smiled back at her.

He could hear them murmuring about the different thread and what color would look good with the quilt top while he helped the younger children pick out their candy.

"Oh, Jonathan, not so much," he heard Delphinia exclaim. She was looking over her shoulder at the twins who had their hands stuffed full of candy.

His attempts to extract the candy from their clenched fists resulted in wails that could be heard throughout the store. Grabbing one under each arm, Jonathan looked over at Delphinia and with a weak smile replied, "Guess I'm not doing my job very well. Think we better get out of here."

"We'll be along in just a few minutes," she called after him.

"Tessie, I think we'd better make our choices soon. Otherwise, your Uncle Jon may be forced to leave without us. I don't think he's feeling particularly patient today," she said as the two women gave each other a knowing smile.

Shortly out of town Jonathan spotted a small grove of trees and pulled over so they could have their picnic. Dinner finished, the twins romped with Joey and Josh while the women discussed getting started on the quilt and the preparations they would need to do for the harvest crew. Jonathan seemed distracted and paid little attention to any of the activity surrounding him, appearing lost in his own thoughts until quite suddenly he said, "Tessie, I'd like to visit with Phiney for a few minutes. Would you mind looking after the children?"

"No, of course not, Uncle Jon," she answered, rising from the blanket where she had been sitting.

As soon as Tessie was out of earshot, Jonathan took Delphinia's hands in his, looked directly in her eyes, and asked, "Have you read your pa's letter yet?"

"No, I'd almost forgotten about it. I planned to read it when we get back home. I thought I had mentioned I was going to wait," she answered with a questioning look as she patted the pocket where she had placed the letter.

"You did. I just thought perhaps you had glanced through

it and had an idea of what he wanted. I'm concerned why he's writing after all this time," Jonathan remarked.

"Do you want me to read it now? In case it's bad news, I didn't want to spoil our trip, but I'll open it if you prefer," she responded.

"No, you wait like you planned. I suppose we really ought to be getting packed up before it gets much later," he answered, starting to gather their belongings and placing them in the wagon.

"You're right," she said, forcing a smile. "Tessie, would you get the children together while I finish packing the food and dishes. We need to be getting started," Delphinia called to the younger woman.

Noting Jonathan's solemn disposition, Delphinia made every attempt to pull him out of his mood. She sang, made jokes with the children, and even tried to get him to join in their word games but her attempts were fruitless and finally, she ceased trying.

Nearing home a light breeze began to blow across the fields of wheat, causing the grain to bend and rise in gentle waves. "Isn't it beautiful, Jonathan? I've never seen the ocean, but my guess would be it looks a lot like that field of wheat, moving in a contented motion to greet the shore," she smiled.

A smile crossed his face as he looked at her. "I never heard anybody get quite so poetic about it, but you're right. It's downright pretty. Almost as pretty as you!"

"Why, Jonathan Wilshire! You keep up that kind of talk and you'll have me blushing."

"Looks to me like you already are," laughed Tessie from the wagon bed as they pulled up in front of the house.

"Tessie, Josh, let's get this wagon unloaded while Phiney gets Joey and the twins ready for bed," Jonathan instructed as he lifted Delphinia down.

With one of the twins on either side and Joey in the lead, they made their way into the house and, without any difficulty, the younger children were in bed and fast asleep.

"I've got to get a few chores done, so I'll be back in shortly," Jonathan advised Delphinia from the doorway.

"Fine," she smiled. "I'll just put a pot of coffee on and it should be ready by the time you're finished."

After Tessie and Josh had gone to bed, Delphinia sat down in the kitchen. She slid her hand into the pocket of her skirt, pulled out the letter, and slowly opened the envelope.

fourteen

Dearest daughter,

I have asked an acquaintance to pen my letter. I hope this finds you well and happy in Kansas. First, I must say I am sorry for not writing you sooner. I know it was thoughtless of me, and in these almost two years, I should have acted more fatherly. However, I can't change what's in the past, and I'm hopeful you don't hold my unkind actions against me.

I wanted you to know I am in Denver City, Colorado, which is not so very far by train. As you know, I had planned on going to California in search of gold, but I stopped in Colorado and never got farther. I don't expect I will, either.

Delphinia, I am dying. The doctor tells me there is no cure for this disease of consumption but. . . .

Reading that dreaded word caused Delphinia's hand to begin shaking, and the sound of Jonathan coming through the door captured her attention.

"What is it?" he asked, seeing the look of horror written on her face.

"It's Pa. He's got consumption," she quietly answered.

"How bad is he?"

"I'm not sure. I haven't finished the letter yet. Here, let me get you some coffee," she said, starting to rise from her chair.

Gently placing his hand on her shoulder, he said, "No, you finish the letter. I'll get us coffee."

Nodding her assent, she lifted the letter back into sight and read aloud.

> "I have implored him to keep me alive so that I may see the face of my darling daughter before I die. He is doing all in his power, practicing his painful bleeding and purging remedies upon me. I am a cooperative patient although at times I feel it would be easier to tell him, 'No more. I shall die now.' If it were not for the fact that I must see you and know you've forgiven me, I would give it up.
>
> "My dearest, darling daughter, I implore you to come to Denver City with all haste so that I may see you before the end comes to me. I have taken the liberty of having a ticket purchased for your departure on the eight o'clock morning train out of Council Grove. You will go north to Junction City and board the Kansas Pacific, which will depart at four-twenty in the evening and arrive in Sheridan at ten the next morning. It will then be necessary for you to embark by stage into Denver City on the United States Express Company Overland Mail and Express Coach. My acquaintance has made all arrangements for your departure on the tenth of July. Your boarding passes will await you at each stop.
>
> "I beg you, please do not disappoint me.
>
> "Your loving father."

They stared silently at each other, the lack of noise deafening in their ears. Finally, Delphinia gave a forced smile and commented, "I wonder who penned that letter for Pa. It certainly was eloquent."

"Somebody else may have thought up the proper words for him, but it's his command. He wants you there. What are you going to do?"

"I don't know. It's just so. . .so sudden. I don't know what to think or what to do. How could I leave now? We've got the harvest crew due here in a week and if I went I don't know how long I'd need to be gone. Who would do all the cooking during harvest? Who would take care of the children? Who would look after everything. It's too much of a burden for Tessie, and yet. . ."

"And yet you're going, isn't that right?" Jonathan queried, knowing his voice sounded harsh.

"He's my father, Jonathan. My only living relative."

"Right. So where was your only living relative when you wanted to stay in Illinois? He was selling you off so he could go live his own dreams. He didn't care about you," he rebutted.

But as soon as the words had been spoken, Jonathan wished he could pull them back into his mouth for he saw the pain they had caused her.

"Oh, Phiney, I'm so very sorry," he said, pulling her into his arms as she burst forth into sobs that racked her body. "I'm criticizing your pa for being selfish and unfeeling and here I am doing the same thing to you."

She buried her head in his shoulder, his shirt turning damp from the deluge of tears. "Please don't cry anymore. You must go to your father. I know that as well as you. I'm just full of regret for waiting so long to declare my love and afraid of losing you just when I felt our lives were beginning."

"You're not losing me. I would be gone for only a short time and then I'd return," she replied.

"I know that's what you think now, but once you get to

Colorado, who knows what will happen. I realize your intentions are to return, but if your father's health is restored and he wants you to stay, or if you meet someone else. . . It's better you leave and make no promises to return."

"That's unfair, Jonathan. You make it sound as though I have no allegiance to my word and that I could not honor an engagement—if you ever asked me to marry," she haughtily answered.

He looked down into her face, feeling such a deep love rise up in him he thought he would die from the thought of losing her. "Phiney, I would be honored to have you as my wife but I'll not ask you for your hand in marriage until you return to Kansas. You're an honest, courageous woman and I know you would make every effort to honor your word, but I'll not try to hamper you in that way. It would be unfair. We'll talk marriage if you return. Right now, we need to talk about getting you ready to leave."

"If that's what you truly want, Jonathan. But we will talk marriage when I return," she answered adamantly.

They talked until late deciding how to accomplish all that needed to be done before Jonathan could take her to Council Grove to meet the train. By the time they had completed their plans, both of them were exhausted. Delphinia bid Jonathan good night from the front porch and, as she watched him walk toward his cabin, her heart was heavy with the thought of leaving this family she had grown to love. Yet deep inside, she ached to once again see her father and knew she must go.

❧

Morning arrived all too soon and both Delphinia and Jonathan were weary, not only from their lack of sleep but from the tasks that lay ahead. The older children uttered their disbelief that Delphinia would even consider leaving, sure they could not exist without her. Amidst flaring tempers and flowing tears, preparations for her departure continued.

Mrs. Aplington agreed to make arrangements with the neighboring farm women to feed the harvest crew and she talked to Jennie O'Laughlin who knew a widow who agreed to come and help care for the children. Delphinia packed her smallest trunk in an effort to assure Jonathan she would not be gone long, and the next morning, after many tears and promises to write, they were on their way to meet the train.

It was a trip filled with a profusion of emotions. Fear of riding the train and meeting a stage by herself, traveling such a great distance, leaving the farm, the children, and man she now loved so dearly, all mixed with the anticipation of seeing her father.

"We've got time to spare. Let's go over to the hotel restaurant and get a hot meal," Jonathan suggested, trying to keep things seeming normal.

The meal smelled delicious but somehow the food would not pass over the lump in her throat and she finally ceased trying. The two of them made small talk, neither saying the things that were uppermost in their minds.

"Better finish up. The train is about ready to pull out. They're loading the baggage," Jonathan remarked.

"I guess I wasn't as hungry as I thought. Let's go ahead and leave," she answered, pushing back the wooden chair, causing it to scrape across the floor.

She waited as Jonathan paid for their meal and slowly they trod toward the waiting train.

"Looks like there's not many passengers so you should be able to stretch out and relax a little," Jonathan stated, trying to keep from pulling her into his arms and carrying her back to his wagon.

She smiled and nodded, knowing that if she spoke at this

moment, her voice would give way to tears and she did not want to cry in front of these strangers.

"Them that's goin', let's get on board," the conductor yelled out.

Jonathan pulled her close and Delphinia felt as though his embrace would crush the life out of her. She tilted her head back and was met by his beautiful blue eyes as he lowered his head and covered her mouth with a tender kiss.

"I love you, Delphinia Elizabeth Hughes, and the day you return, I'll ask you to be my wife," he said as he lifted his head.

"I love you also, Jonathan, and I shall answer 'yes' when you ask for my hand in marriage," she responded, smiling up at him.

He leaned down, kissed her soundly, and then turned her toward the train. "You need to board now. You'll be in our thoughts and prayers," he said as he took hold of her elbow and assisted her up the step and onto the train.

Standing on the platform, he watched as she made her way to one of the wooden seats, trying to memorize every detail of her face for fear he would never see her again.

Peering out the small window, trying to smile as a tear overflowed each eye, she waved her farewell while the train slowly clanked and chugged out of the station, leaving nothing but a billow of dark smoke hanging in the air.

Exhausted from the days of preparation for her trip, Delphinia leaned her head against the window frame and was quickly lulled to sleep by the clacking sounds of the train. She startled awake as the train jerked to a stop and the conductor announced their arrival in Junction City. Gingerly stepping onto the platform, she made her way into the neat, limestone train depot and inquired about her ticket to Sheridan, half expecting to be told they had never heard of her. Instead, the gentlemen handed her a ticket, instructed her as to the whereabouts of a nearby restaurant, and advised her that the train would leave promptly at 4:20 P.M. and that she best not be late.

The information she received was correct. As they pulled out of the station, Delphinia noted it was exactly 4:20 P.M. She found pleasure in the sights as they made their way farther west but as nightfall arrived, she longed to be back at the cabin, getting the children ready for bed and listening to their prayers. They were due to arrive in Sheridan the next morning at ten o'clock but the train was running late, causing Delphinia concern she might miss her stage although the conductor assured her they would arrive in ample time.

Once again, she found her ticket as promised when she arrived at the stage line, although the conductor had been wrong. She had missed the last stage and would have to wait until the next morning. That proved to be a blessing. She was able to make accommodations at the small hotel and even arranged to have a bath in her room. It was heavenly! In fact later she tried to remember just how heavenly that bath had been, sitting cramped on the stage between two men who smelled as though they hadn't been near water in months. The dust and dirt billowed in the windows of the stage, making her even more uncomfortable, but at least she hadn't been forced to eat at the filthy way stations along the route. The hotel owner's wife had warned her of the squalid conditions she would encounter on the trip, counseling Delphinia to take along her own food and water, which had proved to be sound advice.

The trip was long and arduous and when the man beside her said they would soon be arriving in Denver City, she heaved a sigh of relief. The stage rolled into town with the horses at full gallop and then snapped to a stop. Delphinia's head bobbed forward and then lurched back, causing her to feel as though her stomach had risen to her throat and then quickly plummeted to her feet. Not to be denied refreshment at the first saloon, her traveling companions disembarked while the coach was still moving down the dusty street. She almost laughed when the stage driver looked in the door and said, "You plannin' on jest sittin' in there or you gonna get out, ma'am?"

"I thought I'd wait until we came to a full stop," she answered with a slight smile.

"Well, this is about as stopped as we'll be gettin, so better let me give ya a hand," he replied as he reached to assist her down.

"Thank you," she answered, just in time to see the other driver throw her trunk to the ground with a resounding thud.

"You got someone meetin' ya?" he inquired.

"I'm not sure. Perhaps it would be best if you'd move my trunk from the middle of the street into the stage office. I would be most appreciative," she said.

Delphinia was on her way to the office to inquire if her father had left a message when she heard a voice calling her name. Turning, she came face to face with the man who had called out to her.

"Miss Hughes, I'm sorry I'm late. We expected you on the last stage. Your father was so upset when you didn't arrive, that I've had to stay with him constantly. He went to sleep just a little while ago and I didn't notice the time. Please forgive me. The time got away before I realized. I hope you've not been waiting long."

"No. I just arrived," she responded. "But how did you know who I was?"

"Your father told me to look for a beautiful blond with big brown eyes. You fit his description," he answered with a grin.

"I find it hard to believe my father would say I'm beautiful, Mister. . . I'm sorry but I don't know your name."

"It's Doctor. . .Doctor Samuel Finley, at your service, ma'am. And your father did say you are beautiful, you may ask him," he replied.

"You're the doctor my father wrote about? The one that diagnosed and has been treating him for consumption?" she questioned.

"One and the same. I'm also the acquaintance that penned the letter to you and made arrangements for your trip," he advised.

"Well, I suppose my thanks are in order, Dr. Finley. I'm sure my father appreciates your assistance as much as I do. Will you be taking me to my father now?"

"Since he's resting, perhaps you'd like to get settled and refresh yourself."

"If you're sure there's time before he awakens, that would be wonderful," she answered.

Having loaded her trunk, he assisted her into his buggy and after traveling a short distance, they stopped in front of a white frame house with an iron fence surrounding the neatly trimmed yard. Small pink roses were climbing through latticework on each end of the front porch, and neatly trimmed shrubs lined both sides of the brick sidewalk.

"Is this my father's house?" she asked with an astonished look on her face.

"No," he replied. "This is my house. Your father needs almost constant care and since he had no one here to stay with and I'm alone, we agreed this arrangement would be best."

When she did not respond but gave him a questioning look, he continued by adding, "It's really easier for me. I don't have to get out to make house calls since he's right here with me."

"I understand," she answered as he led her into the fashionably appointed parlor, although she was not quite sure she understood anything.

"You just sit down and make yourself at home while I fetch your trunk and then you can get settled," he advised, exiting the front door.

Delphinia watched out the front window as Dr. Finley walked toward the buggy. He was tall, although not as tall as Jonathan, perhaps an inch or two shorter. He had hair that was almost coal black with just a touch of gray at the temples and a slight wave on either side, gray eyes, and the complexion of a man who worked outdoors rather than practiced medicine. His broad shoulders allowed him to carry her trunk with apparent ease and he carried himself with an air of assurance, perhaps bordering on arrogance, Delphinia thought.

She moved away from the window as he entered the house and when he beckoned for her to follow him, she did so without question.

"This is to be your room; I hope you will find it adequate. But if there is anything you need, please let me know. You go ahead and freshen up and I'll check on your father. I promise to let you know as soon as he's awake," he said as he left the room, pulling the door closed behind him.

After washing herself, she unpinned her hair and began to methodically pull the short-bristled brush through the long blond tresses. Leaning back on the tapestry-covered chair, she took note of her surroundings. The walnut dressing table at which she sat was ornately carved with a large oval mirror attached. The bed and bureau were both made of matching walnut and boasted the same ornate carving. All of the windows were adorned with a frilly blue-and-white sheer fabric, the coverlet on the bed matching the blue in the curtains. A beautiful carpet in shades of blue and ivory covered the floor, complementing the other furnishings. It looked opulent and was a startling contrast to the rudimentary conveniences on her journey. She found herself wondering why a doctor would have such a feminine room in his house. Everything, she noted, including the blue-and-white embroidered scarves on the dressing table, emphasized a woman's touch. A knock on the door and Dr. Finley's announcement that her father was awake brought Delphinia's wandering thoughts to an abrupt halt.

fifteen

When Delphinia finally opened the door, Samuel Finely came eye to eye with a beautiful young woman. Her hair, golden and wavy, hung loose to her shoulders, making a wreath around her oval face. The paleness of her skin was accentuated by her deep brown eyes that held just a glint of copper and her lips seemed to have a tiny upward curve with a very slight dimple just above each end of her mouth.

He stood staring at her until Delphinia, not sure what he was thinking, reached toward her hair and remarked, "I guess I was daydreaming. I didn't get my hair pinned up just yet."

"You look absolutely radiant," he replied and smiled as a deep blush colored her cheeks.

"I'll take you to your father now," he said, breaking the silence that followed his compliment.

"Does my father know I've arrived?" she asked, following him down the hallway.

"He does, but try not to look surprised by his appearance when you see him. He's lost weight and his general health is very poor," he responded.

Opening the door for her, he stood back as she brushed by him to enter the room, a distinct scent of lilac filling his nostrils.

"Papa," she almost cried as she made her way to the emaciated figure that lay on the bed, his thin arms outstretched to embrace her.

"Ah, Delphinia, you've let your hair down the way I like it. Come give your papa a hug," he responded in a weakened voice she almost did not recognize. Dr. Finley momentarily watched the unfolding reunion and then quietly backed out the doorway, pulling the door closed behind him.

Her heart ached as she held him, but she forced a bright smile and then said, "I'm not a child anymore, Pa."

"You'll always be my child," he said, reaching up to lay his hand alongside her face. "I know I've done wrong by you and before I die I need your forgiveness for sending you off the way I did. I know now it was selfish and wrong. Say you'll forgive me, Delphinia," he requested in a pleading voice.

"I forgave you long ago, Pa. I was angry when you sent me away and then when I found out you'd gone so far as to advertise in a newspaper to find someplace to send me, I was horrified—"

"I just wasn't—" he interrupted.

"No, Pa. Let me finish. I was shocked and devastated you would do that. Later, though, after some time had passed and I had prayed steadfastly for understanding, I no longer resented your actions. It caused me a lot of pain, but that's behind me now. I've missed you but my life with the Wilshires has been good. You must now concentrate on making yourself well and quit worrying about my forgiveness," she finished.

Tears brimmed his sunken eyes as her father gave a feeble smile. "I don't deserve your forgiveness or love, but I am thankful for both. As for concentrating on getting well, I'm afraid that's not possible. This illness seldom allows its victims to regain their health. Besides, your forgiveness is all I want. Now I don't care when I die," he said, caressing her hand.

"Papa, my forgiveness is not most important," she said. "It's God's forgiveness we must always seek. It is important to ask those we offend to forgive us, but most importantly we must repent and ask God's forgiveness for our sins. I know you used to go to church, but did you accept Jesus as your

Savior and invite Him into your heart? Did you repent and ask God's forgiveness of your sins? Have you tried to live a life that would be pleasing to God? If not, Papa, you're not ready to die and I won't get to see you in heaven. I want us to be together again one day. Just think, you and Mama and me, together in heaven," she said, not sure how he would react to her intonation.

"You're a lot like your mama, young lady," he said. "Maybe you're right and I have been looking in the wrong direction for my forgiveness. You continue to pray for me and I'll ask for some forgiveness. It probably wouldn't hurt for me to have a talk with the preacher," he said and then broke into a spasm of racking coughs.

Hearing the sound, Dr. Finley entered the room just as Delphinia rose from her chair to fetch him.

"Don't worry. This is common with his illness. Why don't you let him rest a while. Sometimes talking causes these bouts to come on, but it will cease shortly," he reassured her. "Why don't you take a few minutes and relax outside. We'll be having dinner soon."

Sitting on one of the two rockers that faced each other on the front porch, Delphinia uttered a prayer of thankfulness for her father's receptive attitude to their conversation about God. As she finished her prayer, Dr. Finley walked out the door and sat down in the chair opposite her.

"He's doing fine," he said in answer to the questioning look she gave him.

"Is there anything I can do to assist? I'm a decent cook and would be happy to help," she offered.

"Well, I thank you kindly but I'm afraid my neighbor, Mrs. O'Mallie, might take offense. She's been cooking for me ever since my wife passed away. She likes making the extra money and I like having a warm meal. She looks after your pa when I have to be gone on calls, and she even does my laundry. Her husband passed away a week after my wife, Lydia, so we've been a help to each other," he responded.

"I'm sorry about your wife," she said, not sure how to react to his casual declaration of her death.

"Don't be. She suffered from severe mental depression after the death of our baby and never got over it. Several months after the baby died, she contracted typhoid and was actually happy about it. She wanted to die. It's been eight years now and I've made my peace with the situation," he responded, giving her a slight smile.

"And you never remarried?" Delphinia asked, realizing too late that her question was intrusive and wishing she could take it back.

Dr. Finley burst into laughter as he watched how uncomfortable the young woman had become once she issued her question.

"No," he replied. "I've never met the right woman, although I believe that may have changed several hours ago. Your father told me what a beautiful, high-spirited daughter he had, but I thought it was the usual boasting of a proud parent. I find he spoke the truth and I couldn't be more delighted."

Disconcerted by the doctor's remarks, Delphinia began pressing down the pleats in her skirt with the palm of her hand in a slow, methodical motion. "I'm sure my pa told you of my temper and feisty behavior, also," she replied, trying to make light of the compliments.

"I believe he did, at that," he answered and gave a chuckle. "Looks like Mrs. O'Mallie is on her way to the back door with dinner. I better go meet her," he said as he bounded out of the chair and into the house.

Later, lying in bed, Delphinia reflected upon the events of the day. Exhausted, she had unpacked only what was necessary for the night and then had fallen into bed, sure she would be asleep before finishing her prayers. But instead of sleep, her mind kept wandering back to the conversation on the front porch with Dr. Finley. During dinner he had insisted that she call him Sam and he had certainly made her feel at home. Yet she was not sure how to take some of the remarks he made, nor how much her pa had told him about why she lived in Kansas.

❧

The next week passed quickly. Sam was always there, willing to help in any way she asked. He arranged for the preacher to visit with her father, posted her letters, insisted on showing her around town, and still maintained a thriving medical practice. Most of the time she spent with her father and when she would mention returning to Kansas, he would beg her to remain until his death.

Toward the beginning of the second week she confided in Sam that she planned to leave within the next few days.

"I'd rethink that decision. If you leave, I'm sure it will break your father's heart," he said, knowing he was arguing as much for himself as he was for her father.

"But you've told me he may live for a month or longer. I couldn't possibly wait that long," she argued, feeling selfish. "Besides, I told the Wilshires I would be gone for only a few weeks at the most," she continued, trying to defend her position, his statements adding to her guilt.

She was torn by uncertainty, feeling that she would fail someone, no matter what. Her prayers had been fervent about where she belonged, but no answer had been forthcoming, at least none that she could discern. She hadn't even unpacked all her clothing, fearing she would begin to feel settled.

As the days passed and her indecision continued, Sam and her father felt assured that she would remain in Denver City. She accompanied Sam to several socials at the church and he proved to be an enjoyable companion, making her realize that city life held a certain appeal. But she found herself missing Jonathan and the children. The letters she received from them were cheerful and told of missing her, but not to worry about them. They did not ask when she would return, and she did not mention it in her letters to them.

Delphinia's father watched out the window by his bed as she and Sam came up the sidewalk returning from an evening stroll, her arm laced through his. Her father gave a slight smile as they stepped out of his sight and onto the porch.

"Let's sit here on the porch and visit a while, if you're not too tired," Sam invited.

"How could I be tired?" she bantered. "I do nothing but sit all day."

"You're growing restless, aren't you? I could sense it all day," he responded.

"Sam, I'm used to hard work and keeping busy. I've been caring for five children and a homestead out on the Kansas prairie. I miss the children and I guess I miss the work, too," she admitted.

"You're far too beautiful to work on a farm. There's no need for you to return to that kind of life. You should be living in a city, married, and having children of your own. Don't you want to have your own children?" he asked.

"Of course I want to have my own children, but that doesn't cause me to love or miss the Wilshires any the less. You say there's no need to return to that kind of life. My father doesn't have much longer to live by your calculations and once he's gone, I'll have no one but my substitute family in Kansas. I think that is where I belong," she stated.

Reaching toward her he took hold of her hand and lifted it to his lips, gently placing a kiss in the center of her palm. "No, Delphinia, you belong here with me. I care for you more than you can imagine. I have from the first day you arrived."

"Oh, Jonathan. . .I. . .I mean, Samuel," she stammered. "I think I had better retire," she said, rising from the chair and moving toward the front door.

"So I do have competition. It's not just the children you miss. Are you in love with this Kansas farmer?" he asked, blocking her entry to the house.

"I. . .well, I think so," she finally answered.

The last word had barely passed her lips when he drew her into his arms and kissed her with an impatient fervor that almost frightened her.

"Please, don't. I must check on my father," she said, entering the house and leaving him on the front porch.

&

"I wasn't sure if you'd still be awake, Pa," Delphinia said, approaching his bedside.

"You two have a nice walk?"

"Why, uh, I guess so. Yes, it's a pleasant evening. I wish you could be outdoors a while and enjoy it with me," she answered, trying to hide her emotions over the recent incident with Sam.

"I get a nice breeze through the window. Sometimes I even hear people talkin' on the porch," he said with a grin.

She did not respond but began to tidy the room and straighten his sheets.

"He's a good man, Delphinia. You couldn't ask for a better catch to marry up with. I know he's thinkin' hard on the prospect of asking you 'cause he asked if I'd have any objection," her father continued.

Her head jerked to attention at his remark. "What did you tell him?" she asked, her voice sounding harsh to her ears.

"I didn't mean to upset you. I thought you'd be happy to know he was interested in you. I told him I didn't know anyone I'd be more pleased to have marry my daughter, but he'd have to take it up with you," he answered, seeing that she was disturbed by the conversation.

"Pa, I'm not looking for a prize catch. I'm not even looking for a husband. The only reason I came to Denver City was to see you and then I'll be returning to Kansas. In fact, I should have returned a week ago," she responded.

"Now, I've gone and made you unhappy and you're gonna run off and leave me here to die alone, aren't ya?" he asked, hoping her tender heart would not allow her to rush off in anger.

"You've not made me unhappy, Pa. I know you're thinking about my future, but I've been on my own for some time now and I don't need anyone making marriage plans for me. Besides, Jonathan Wilshire has pledged his love and intent to marry me once I return to Kansas," she told him as she rearranged the small bottles on a nearby table for the third time.

"Those bottles look fine; you've straightened them enough. Now come and sit down here," he said, indicating the chair beside him.

"Delphinia, I'll not try and push you into any marriage. Folks need to marry those they love. I know that. I loved your ma like I could never love anyone else. But there's a lot to be said for finding the person you're suited to. It makes things run smoother."

"I know that. But I think Jonathan and I are suited," she answered.

"Maybe so. I thought you're ma and I were, too. I tried to make her happy but she longed for city life and even though I helped her as much as I could, it was a hard life. She always wanted the kind of life she'd had as a child, but she gave in to my dreams and left it behind. I'm not sure she ever got over leaving her family," he continued.

"She wasn't unhappy and you know it, Pa. We both know she would have preferred living in the East, close to her family, but she understood."

"I was married to her, child. You saw what she wanted you to see. But many's the night I listened to her cry about life out in the middle of nowhere and longin' to see her family and lead a city life. I'm real sorry I did that to her," he said, a distant look in his eyes.

"You did the best you could," Delphinia answered, not knowing what to say that would relieve some of his pain.

"That's true. I did. The only thing I could have done different would have been to stay in the city. You got that chance to stay now. It's what your ma would have wanted for you and here you are with this wonderful opportunity. Denver's not like those big eastern cities, but it's an up and coming kind of town. One day it's gonna be grand, for sure," he boasted.

"That was Ma who wanted the big city. I've never said that."

"Perhaps, but you could have a good life here. You're too young to be tied down to somebody else's children. Doc Finley's a fine man and he could take care of you. You'd never want for anything and you could eventually have children of your own. You'd be able to give them what they needed without worrying about money," he said, beginning to cough from the exertion of talking so much.

"That's enough for tonight, Pa. You're getting excited and you're going to make yourself worse. I'm going to get your medicine ready and then I want you to get some rest," she said as she moved toward the bottles and poured out a spoonful of the yellow liquid.

"I'll take the medicine and go to sleep if you promise to think on what we've talked about," he responded and then clenched his mouth together like a small child.

Looking at his face she was unable to hold back her laughter. "It's a deal. Now open up," she said as she cradled his head and lifted him to take the spoon.

She leaned down and placed a kiss on his cheek. "Good night, Papa. I love you."

Smiling, he bid her good night with the admonition she think hard on his words. She smiled and nodded her assent as she left the room and pulled the door closed behind her.

"How is he?" Sam asked.

Delphinia jumped at the sound of his voice. "You startled me. I thought you'd gone to bed," she said, turning to find him sitting on the stairway outside her father's bedroom. "He's doing pretty well. He got a bit excited and talked too much, which caused his cough to start up. I just gave him his medicine and hopefully he'll get a good night's rest," she answered.

"I want to apologize for my behavior this evening. I didn't mean to offend you. I care for you very much and it's been difficult for me not to kiss you before now," he stated.

"Perhaps this is something we should talk about another time. I'm really very tired," she answered and moved toward her bedroom.

"Whenever you're ready, my love," he said, going up the stairway.

Quickly, she make her way down the hallway to her bedroom, but could not deny the small flutter she felt when he used the term of endearment.

She lay in bed thinking of the things both her pa and Sam had said. *I do want children of my own and I wonder if I'll grow weary of raising my Kansas family and never really have time for my own,* she thought.

Tossing restlessly, she questioned the excitement she felt when Dr. Finley had called her by a term of endearment.

"Can I be in love with Jonathan and still feel something for another man?" she whispered to herself.

That night her prayers were fervent for God's direction.

sixteen

Delphinia awakened to a day that had dawned bright and sunny with a crispness to the air, giving notice that summer was over. Just as she finished making her bed, she heard the back door slam and Mrs. O'Mallie enter the kitchen.

"I'll be right there to help you, Mrs. O'Mallie," she called out.

"Take your time. I'm in no hurry," the older woman answered.

"Here, let me take that tray," she offered, reaching toward the huge silver platter and placing it on the kitchen table.

"It's a beauty of a day out there and I've been thankin' the Lord for that. Don't want anything to spoil our meeting tonight," she said.

"You have special plans for today?" Delphinia inquired hospitably.

"Why, sure. It's the autumn revival. Thought maybe Doc Finley might have mentioned it. All the churches get together and have one big revival each fall. It's going be wonderful. There's a service every night this week so if your pa is doing all right, I hope you'll come," she invited.

"I'd love to, but I'll have to see how he's feeling later this afternoon. Thank you for telling me about it," Delphinia answered.

"Well, guess I better be gettin' back home. You give thought to coming tonight," Mrs. O'Mallie said, leaving out the back door.

"Looks like Mrs. O'Mallie's already been here and gone," Sam said as he entered the kitchen.

"She just left. I'll take Pa's tray to him. You go ahead and eat," she responded.

"I'll wait for you," he answered as she left the room.

"There's no need to do that," she answered, walking out of the kitchen before he could respond.

"Good morning, Pa. How are you feeling today?" she inquired, thinking he looked thinner each day.

"Not too bad, but I'm not hungry. You go eat. I'll try and eat later," he responded. But seeing the look of determination on his daughter's face, he shook his head and said, "I'm not going to eat now, so you needn't argue with me. Go!"

"All right, all right," she answered with a smile. "I'm going.

"He's not hungry," she announced, walking into the kitchen and sitting down opposite Sam at the wooden table.

"Don't look so downcast. That doesn't necessarily mean anything bad. We all have times when we're not hungry. Looks to me like you'd better quit worrying about your pa's eating and take a nap this afternoon. Those dark circles under your eyes tell me you didn't get much sleep last night."

"You're right, I didn't. I'll think about the nap if you'll tell me about the revival," she said.

"Revival? How'd you hear about that?" he questioned.

"Mrs. O'Mallie told me. I'd love to go if Pa is all right. Do you think that would be possible?" she asked.

He smiled as he watched her face become animated and bright, like a child seeing a jar of peppermint sticks.

"There's really nothing to tell. Several years ago the churches here in Denver City decided to have one big revival each autumn. They all get together and select a preacher to come and they hold services outdoors every night. If the weather doesn't cooperate, they go over to the Methodist Church, since it's the biggest. I don't see any reason why you couldn't go, but not unescorted since it's held during the evening," he responded.

"Perhaps I could go with Mrs. O'Mallie," she suggested.

"If your pa's doing all right, I'll escort you," he said, "at least this one evening, but you must promise to rest this afternoon."

"I will," she answered delightedly. "Our breakfast is probably cold. Do you want to give thanks?" she asked.

"You go ahead and do it for us," he answered.

"Mrs. O'Mallie certainly knows how to start off the day with a hearty breakfast," he said, having devoured all that was on his plate and wiping his hands with the large cloth napkin. "I'd better get busy on my house calls. Don't forget your pa's medicine this morning and I expect you to be taking a nap when I return," he admonished.

"Oh, I will be," she answered, excited by the prospect of the evening.

"Guess what, Papa," she exclaimed, almost skipping into his room.

"I don't know what to guess except that something has made you happy," he ventured.

"There's a revival beginning tonight and Sam said that if you're doing all right this evening and if I take a nap this afternoon, he'll escort me. Isn't that wonderful?"

"Well, it certainly is wonderful and I'll be doing just fine. You just be sure and get that nap and find yourself something to wear," he said, pleased to see her so happy about going out with Sam.

"Something to wear. Oh, yes. I'd not even thought of that. I'll need to look in my trunk and see if I can find something extra special. Oh, and then I'll need to get it pressed. I'd better get that done or I'll not have my nap taken before Sam returns," she said.

"You get a move on then. I'm feeling fine and I'll ring the bell if I need anything," he said.

He waved her out of the room as she blew him a kiss and headed toward the doorway. *Perhaps she's decided that Sam would be the right man for her, after all,* he thought, pleased by the prospect.

Delphinia lifted the lid on the partially empty trunk. She still hadn't completely unpacked the contents. *I hope I packed something warmer in the bottom of this trunk,* she thought, methodically removing each item. Lifting a dark gold dress, her eyes flew open at the fabric tucked within the folds of the dress. It was Sarah's quilt top! And there, underneath the dress was a neatly folded piece of paper. She sat down on the edge of the bed and slowly opened the page.

> *Dear Phiney,*
> *While you were busy with the twins, I packed Mama's quilt top in with your dress. I want you to come back to Kansas. I didn't know how else to be sure of your return. I'm hoping the threads of love in this quilt are strong enough to bring you home to us.*
>
> *Love,*
> *Tessie*

Tears rolled down her cheeks as she read the letter a second time. The words tugged at her heart and made her even more lonely for Kansas and the family she had left behind. *I've got to make a decision soon,* she thought, folding the letter and placing it with the quilt top in her trunk. *Surely God will give me an answer soon.*

She carried her dress into the kitchen, searching until she found a pressing board and then heated the iron. Carefully she pressed the gown, watchful not to burn the silk fabric. Certain all the wrinkles had been removed, she draped it over a chair in her bedroom and took the promised nap.

Later, she could hardly wait for dinner to be over in order to clear off the dishes and get ready. Sam had declared her father was doing fine and they would leave in an hour. She took her time getting ready, pinning her hair up on top of her head, and then securing it with a thin, black and gold ribbon. A white lace collar surrounded the neckline of her dress and she placed a gold earring in each lobe. Looking at her reflection in the mirror above the walnut bureau, she remembered that the last time she had worn the earrings had been when Pastor Martin escorted her to the dance. She smiled thinking about that night when Jonathan had become their uninvited guest. It seemed so long ago, almost a different world, she mused.

"You about ready? You're pa wants to see you before we leave. I'll wait in his room," Sam said, knocking on the door.

"Be right there," she answered. Taking one last look in the mirror, she pinned a wisp of hair and then went to her father's room.

Her entry brought raves from her father who insisted that she twirl around several times so he could see her from all angles. Sam was silent, although she could feel his eyes on her from the moment she entered the room.

"We'd better leave or we'll be late," he said, rising from the chair.

"Are you sure you'll be okay, Pa?"

"I'm sure. Now you two go on and have a nice time," he instructed.

Sam had drawn his carriage to the front of the house and carefully assisted her into the buggy, his two black horses appearing sleek in the semidarkness.

"You look quite beautiful. I didn't want to tell you in front of your father for fear of causing you embarrassment. Besides, it would have been difficult to get a word in," he said, smiling down at her.

"Fathers tend to think their daughters are beautiful, no matter what," she responded.

"Perhaps. But in your case it's true," he answered as he pulled himself into the buggy and flicked the reins.

"How far is it to the meeting place?" she asked, wanting to change the subject.

"Not far, just south of town. There's a large grove and they set up benches and chairs, whatever they can move from the churches. There's been ample seating when I've been there," he commented.

The crowd had already begun to gather by the time they arrived. Mrs. O'Mallie had saved seats, hopeful they would attend. She was in the third row, waving them forward with unbridled enthusiasm.

"Oh, there's Mrs. O'Mallie. Come on, Sam, we can sit up front. She's saved seats," Delphinia pointed out, tugging his arm.

"I'd rather sit farther back, if it's all the same to you," he answered, holding back.

"Oh," she said, somewhat surprised, "that's fine. I'll just go tell Mrs. O'Mallie. Why don't you see if you can find a spot for us."

The older woman was disappointed and Delphinia would have much preferred to sit up front, but deferred to Sam's choice since he had been kind enough to escort her.

The services were all that Delphinia had hoped for. The preacher was dynamic and the crowd was receptive to his message. They sang songs, read Scripture, and heard the Word preached, and when the service was over, Delphinia could hardly wait to return for the next evening.

"Wasn't it wonderful?" she asked Sam as they made their way to the buggy.

"It was interesting," he responded, saying nothing further.

Delphinia was so excited about the meeting, she did not

note how quiet Sam had been, nor the fact that he had little to say the whole way home.

When they finally reached the porch, she said, "Do you think we could go tomorrow?" She sounded so full of anticipation. He thought once again of a child being offered candy.

"I don't think so," he answered, watching as her face became void of the animation it had held just minutes before.

"Why? Do you think it unwise to leave Pa again?" she asked.

"No, that's not why. I think one night of observation is sufficient," he answered.

"Observation? What an odd thing to say. Attending church or revival is not something one observes. It's something you do. It's worshiping God," she said, looking at him through a haze of confusion.

"Not for me," he responded.

"Whatever do you mean, Sam? You believe in God. You've accepted Jesus as your Savior. . .haven't you?" she asked, doubt beginning to creep into her thoughts.

"I attend church because it's the respectable thing to do and people expect it of a doctor. As for your question, however, the answer is no, I don't believe in God."

With that pronouncement, Delphinia almost fell onto the chair just behind her and stared at him in open-mouthed disbelief.

"I'm sure that comes as a shock to you, but I consider myself an educated man. I believe in science and have studied in some of the best schools in this country and Europe. There is absolutely nothing to support the theory of your God, Delphinia. I realize most people have a need to believe in some higher being and so they cling to this God and Jesus ideology. I don't need it. I believe in myself and when life is over, it's over," he said, sitting down opposite her.

"But, but, you've acted as though you believe. You went

and got the pastor for my father and you attend church and you talk to Mrs. O'Mallie about God and you pray—"

"No," he interrupted, "I do not pray. I allow others to pray over their food and I discuss God with Mrs. O'Mallie because she enjoys talking about such things. You have never heard me pray, and you won't. When a dying patient wants a preacher, I see to it. That doesn't mean I think it's needed," he answered.

"I don't know what to say. I just can't believe you're saying this," she said, rising from the chair and pacing back and forth. "I know you place great value in your education, but I hope you'll heed the words of 1 Corinthians 3:18 where it tell us that if any man seems to be wise in this world, let him become a fool so he may become wise," she said, hoping he would listen, but realizing from his vacant stare that he did not care to hear.

"I've heard that rhetoric preached all my life. My parents took me to church every Sunday. My mother was devout, although my father confided in later years that he never believed, but for my mother's sake, he acted like he believed," he said.

When she did not respond, he continued, "I wanted you to know how I felt before we marry. I'll not stop you from attending church, and on occasion I'll escort you. But I'll not want you there all the time, nor would I want our children indoctrinated with such nonsense," he added.

"Before we marry? I never said I would marry you. I never even gave you cause to think that," she fired back at him.

"I never doubted you would accept. I realize how much I have to offer a woman. A nice home, security, I'm kind, and, I've been told, good looking," he said with a smile.

"I'm sure to many women those would be the most important qualities, but your confidence in my acceptance is unfounded. I would never marry a man who didn't believe in Jesus Christ as his Savior. I feel sorry for you, Sam, if you've hardened your heart against the Lord, but I want you to know I'll be praying for you," she said, walking toward her father's room.

"I think I'd better check on my father and get ready for bed. Good night, Sam."

"Good night, Delphinia. I've not accepted what you said as your final word, however. We'll discuss this further tomorrow," he answered, not moving from the chair.

Her father was fast asleep when she stepped into his room. She backed out quietly and made her way down the hall to prepare for bed.

Sitting at the dressing table, she gazed at the reflection of herself. *How could I have been so blind?* She forced herself to think back over the weeks she had lived in this house. It was true, she had never seen Sam pray. At meals he always deferred to someone else and now that she thought about it, whenever she would pray with her father, he would leave the room. When she had tried to discuss the sermons they had heard on Sundays or ask his opinion about a verse of Scripture, he would always change the subject.

She slipped into her nightgown and dropped to her knees beside the bed and earnestly thanked God for answered prayer, certain His intent was for her to return to Kansas and be joined with a godly man. She prayed regularly for those she loved and tonight she added a prayer for the salvation of Dr. Samuel Finley, an educated man, walking in darkness.

ã

Arising the next morning, Delphinia hastened to get herself dressed, wanting to talk with her father. Sam was waiting in the kitchen when she entered and requested she join him for breakfast.

"I'd rather not this morning. I'm not very hungry and I'd like to visit with my father. I didn't spend much time with him yesterday and we need to talk," she said, lifting the tray of food and moving toward the door.

"We will talk later," he said tersely.

"There is no doubt about that," she answered emphatically, without looking back.

Who does he think he is? she thought, marching down the hallway to her father's room. She stopped before entering, knowing she must change her attitude before seeing him and taking a moment to issue a short prayer that God assist her in this discussion.

"Good morning, Papa," she greeted, smiling brightly.

"Good morning to you," he said, indicating the chair by his bed. "Sit and tell me all about your evening."

"I plan to do just that, but first you must eat," she told him, lifting a napkin off the tray and placing an extra pillow behind him.

"I'll eat while you talk. Have we got a deal?" he asked.

"As long as you eat, I'll talk," she said, glad to see a little more color in his cheeks.

He lifted a small forkful of food to his mouth and nodded at her to begin.

"Papa, I know you have a desire for me to marry Sam and he has asked for my hand."

"I'm glad to hear that, Delphinia. When's the weddin' to be? Maybe, I'll be well enough to attend," he said excitedly.

"There won't be a wedding. At least not a wedding between Sam and me," she answered.

"What do you mean? You're confusing me," he said, slapping the fork on his tray.

"There's no need to get upset. I'm going to explain, if you'll just eat and let me talk," she admonished. "Sam has asked for my hand but I could never marry a man unless he's a Christian. Sam doesn't believe in God. Besides, Papa, I don't love Sam. I love Jonathan Wilshire. I have to admit that I was swayed by Sam's good looks and kind ways and that it was nice to be escorted about the city and have his attention. But that's not love. A marriage between us would be doomed for failure."

"You can't be sure of that. You just said he's good and kind and you enjoy his company. I don't want you livin' out your days workin' like your mama, always unhappy and wishin' for more," he said.

"Just because Mama was unhappy some of the time doesn't mean she would have changed things. She loved you, Pa, and that's where a woman belongs. With the man she loves. You've got to understand that I could never love Sam. Not unless he turned to the Lord, and then I'm not sure. He's hardened his heart against God. Why, he told me he wouldn't even allow his children to be brought up as Christians. You know I couldn't turn my back on God like that," she responded adamantly.

"I understand what you're saying and I know you're right. I guess I'm just being selfish again. I want you to have all the things I could never give your mother, even if you don't want them."

"Don't you see, she had the most important things: a family that loved her and the love of our Savior. That's all any of us really need to be happy," she said, leaning down and placing a kiss on his cheek.

seventeen

When Sam returned later in the afternoon, Delphinia was sitting on the front porch, enjoying the cool breeze and silently thanking God for the afternoon discussion with her father and his agreement that she return to Kansas.

"I thought you'd be in tending to your father," Sam said with no other greeting.

"I just came out. He's asleep and I wanted some fresh air," she answered defensively.

"Good, then we can have our talk," he rebutted, sitting down and moving the chair closer.

"There's really nothing further to say, Sam. I can't marry you. I've explained that I could never marry a non-Christian and besides, I'm in love with Jonathan Wilshire," she said, leaning back in her chair in an effort to place a little more distance between them.

"As I recall, you weren't quite so sure of your love for that Wilshire fellow when I kissed you on this very porch."

"I'm not going to defend myself or my actions to you, but I hope you'll believe and accept my decision in this matter. It will make life easier for all three of us," she responded, hoping to ease the tension between them.

"I think your pa will have something to say about this. I've already asked for your hand and he as much as promised it. So you see, the decision really hasn't been made yet," he answered with a smug look on his face.

"I've discussed the matter fully with my father, Sam. He is in agreement that I should follow my heart and return to Kansas. He was unaware of your disbelief in God, as much

148

as I was. There is no doubt in his mind that I could not be happily married to a non-Christian. The Bible warns Christians about being unequally yoked."

"Don't start quoting Scripture to me. That's the last thing I want to hear. What I want to know is how you talked your father into allowing you to return to Kansas?" he interrupted.

"I've already explained and he realizes the folly of my marrying someone like you. He may have discussed the fact that he thought a marriage between us would be good, but you deceived him, too. I'm not sure it was intentional, since you find faith in God so unimportant. I would rather believe you didn't set out to mislead either of us. I'd prefer you didn't upset my father by discussing this further, but you're the doctor. Do as you see fit," she said, hearing the small bell at her father's bedside and rising to go to his room.

"Stay here. I'll see to him," Sam said, standing and picking up his bag.

She did not move from the chair, but it was not long before Sam returned. Leaning against the thick rail that surrounded the porch, he looked down at her, his eyes filled with sadness.

"We could be happy, you know. If I'm willing to overlook your foolish beliefs and allow you to practice your Christian rituals, why is it so difficult for you to think our marriage wouldn't work?" he asked.

"That's exactly why—because you don't believe. It would always be a struggle between us. I want to be able to share my love of the Lord with my husband and raise my children to know God. I want God to be the head of our house and that could never happen if I were married to you," she answered.

"You've done a good job of convincing your father. I found no allegiance from him when we talked. I guess there's nothing more to say, except that I love you and if you change your mind, we can forget this conversation ever took place," he said and walked in the house.

Delphinia remained, not wanting to discuss the matter further. When she was sure Sam had gone upstairs, she went to her father's room.

"I wondered if you'd gone to bed without a good night kiss for me," he said, watching her enter the room.

"No, I'd not do that," she replied, straightening the sheet and pulling the woolen blanket up around his chest. "How are you feeling this evening?"

"Not too bad," he answered. "I talked with Sam."

"I know. He told me," she said, sitting down beside him.

"He's not happy with either of us. Maybe one day he'll open his heart to the Lord. If not, I suppose someday he may find a woman who thinks as he does. I have something I'd like for you to do tomorrow," he said, taking her hand.

"I'll try," she answered.

"I want you to go to town," he instructed, pulling a small leather pouch from beneath his pillow. "I'd like for you to purchase your wedding gown here in Denver City. I know I can't attend the ceremony, but it would give me great pleasure to see you in your wedding dress. Would you consider doing that?"

"You don't need to spend your money on a wedding gown, Pa. I have a dress that will do," she answered.

"Always trying to look out for everyone else, aren't ya? I can afford to buy you a dress and it would give me great pleasure. Now, will you do that for me? Mrs. O'Mallie has agreed to go with you. Quite enthusiastically, I might add," he said with a smile.

"If it would please you, I'll go shopping with Mrs. O'Mallie. Did you and Mrs. O'Mallie decide when this shopping trip is to take place?" she inquired, plumping his pillow.

"Tomorrow morning, just as soon as the shops are open. She said she'd come over for you and I told her you'd be ready," he answered.

"Pretty sure of yourself, were you?" she asked, letting out a chuckle.

"I know you pretty well, girl. You wouldn't deny an old man his dying wish."

"Don't talk like that, please," she said, shaking her head.

"It's better to face up to the facts. We both know I've not long for this world. You mustn't get sad on me. After all, it's you who gave me hope, knowing I'd be seeing you and your mother again one day. You just keep thinking on that and forget this dying business," he said and then waved his hand, gesturing her to leave the room. "You get off to bed now. You need your rest for all that shopping you're going to do tomorrow, and I need my sleep."

She leaned down and placed a kiss on his cheek. "I'll stop in before I go tomorrow. You sleep well," she said, departing for her own room.

⋯

Delphinia took care in dressing, wanting to look her best when she visited the shops in Denver City. Just as she was tying on her bonnet, Frances O'Mallie arrived. The older woman was so excited at the prospect of purchasing a wedding dress, she talked nonstop from the time she entered the house until they reached the door of the first small shop.

The store owner was a lovely woman, delighted to see her first customers of the day. It was immediately obvious to her that these women were going to make purchases, and she needed the business. Mrs. O'Mallie instantly took charge, asking to see what fabrics and laces the woman had in stock, fingering each item with a knowledge that surprised Delphinia. Taking her assignment seriously, the older woman inquired about how long it would take to make the dress, how many yards of fabric for each of the patterns they had viewed, and the exact cost for everything from the tiny buttons to the lace trimming. Just when the clerk was sure the women were ready to make their decision, Mrs. O'Mallie took Delphinia by the elbow and said, "Come, my dear, we must check the other stores."

Opening the door to exit, she informed the store owner, "We'll be back, unless we find something more to our liking."

Delphinia, somewhat stunned by Mrs. O'Mallie's actions, was quick to tell her she particularly liked one of the patterns and wanted to discuss it further.

"Tut, tut, don't you worry. These merchants always need business, and it's good to know what the competition has to offer," she said, ushering Delphinia into a shop with beautiful gold lettering on the windows proclaiming the finest needlework west of the Mississippi.

"Lucy Blodgett owns this place," Mrs. O'Mallie whispered. "She can be real hard to deal with, but her sign on the window is true. She does the finest needlework I've ever seen. Just let me do the talking," she instructed.

The brass bell over the front door announced their entry and the women observed Lucy Blodgett making her way from the back room of the shop.

"Mornin', Lucy. This is Delphinia Hughes. She's out here from Kansas looking for a wedding dress and I told her you do the handsomest needlework in these parts," Mrs. O'Mallie praised.

"Good morning to you, Frances. Nice to make your acquaintance, Miss Hughes. Why don't you ladies come back and have a seat. I find it much more expeditious to discuss just what my customer is here for, and then proceed to show you my line of goods," she smiled, leading them toward four elegant walnut chairs that encircled a matching table.

Flitting through patterns that were neatly stacked on a shelf, she produced five different styles. "Why don't you look at these while I get us some tea," she offered.

"She knows how to run a business, wouldn't you say?" Mrs. O'Mallie asked, thoroughly enjoying the opulent surroundings.

"It would appear that way, but are you sure this shop isn't too expensive?" Delphinia questioned.

"We'll see, we'll see," the older woman replied, pushing the patterns toward the younger woman. "I rather like this one."

"Here we are, tea and some biscuits," Miss Blodgett said, placing a tray in the middle of the table. "Why don't you pour for us, Frances, and I'll visit with Miss Hughes."

Mrs. O'Mallie was glad to oblige. The silver tea service and china cups seemed exactly what should be used while discussing wedding gowns with Miss Lucy Blodgett. Delphinia's escort sat back and had her tea and biscuits, not missing a word that passed between the other women.

"How long would it take for you to complete the gown?" Delphinia asked, having finally settled on one of the patterns.

"At a minimum, three weeks. I have many orders to fill and once I give my word that a purchase will be ready, I am never late. Isn't that right, Frances?"

"Absolutely," said Mrs. O'Mallie, wiping the crumbs from her mouth and taking a swallow of tea.

"Well, I'm sorry to have taken your time, Miss Blodgett, but I must leave for Kansas within the week. My father wanted me to purchase a gown here in Denver City so he might see it before I depart. It appears that isn't going to be possible," Delphinia said, rising from the chair.

"I'm sorry, too, Miss Hughes. You're a lovely young woman and I could make you into a beautiful bride,"

Miss Blodgett replied.

"You'll not find a seamstress in this city who can make you a wedding gown within the week, I'm sorry to say," she continued as Mrs. O'Mallie and Delphinia tied their bonnets, preparing to leave.

"We appreciate your time, Lucy," Mrs. O'Mallie said as they walked out the store and walked toward another shop down the street.

The two women had walked as far as the livery stable when they heard Lucy Blodgett calling, and observed her motioning them to return.

"Lucy Blodgett, I've never seen you make such a spectacle of yourself," Mrs. O'Mallie said, feigning surprise.

"I've been making a fool of myself for years, Frances. At least whenever I felt there was cause to do so," she answered with a smile.

"Come back in the shop. I just may be able to solve your problem, Miss Hughes," she said, leading Delphinia to the rear of the store and into her workroom.

"Stand right here," she said, placing Delphinia along the wall opposite her cutting table. Moving across the room, Miss Blodgett walked to a closet and removed a hanger that was draped with a sheet. In one dramatic swoop, she pulled off the sheet revealing a beautiful white gown that absolutely took Delphinia's breath away.

"Oh, Miss Blodgett, it's beautiful. . .truly beautiful," Delphinia said, staring at the creation. Walking toward the dress, she reached out and touched the tiny beads that had been sewn in an intricate pattern on the bodice. The long sleeves were made of a delicate lace that matched the overlay of the floor-length skirt, flowing into a short train.

"It appears to be just about your size, I would guess," Miss Blodgett replied, ignoring the compliment.

"Perhaps a mite big," Mrs. O'Mallie responded.

"Well, certainly nothing a good seamstress couldn't remedy in short order," the shop owner replied rather curtly.

"What difference does it make?" Delphinia interrupted, exasperated that the two women were arguing over alterations on a wedding dress that had been made for another bride.

"That's why I called you back to the shop," Miss Blodgett responded, looking at Delphinia as if she were dimwitted. "This dress is available."

"Available? How could it be available?" she asked, stunned by the remark.

"I hesitate to tell you why for fear you'll not want the dress, but with all the folks Mrs. O'Mallie knows, I'm sure she'd find out soon enough anyway. This is the dress I made for Mary Sullivan's daughter, Estelle," Miss Blodgett began.

"Ah, yes," Mrs. O'Mallie said, nodding her head in recognition.

"Estelle Sullivan was to be married last Sunday afternoon. Her intended made a little money mining for gold, but his claim went dry. They decided to settle in California so he went out in June to look at some possible investments. Two weeks before the wedding, she got a letter saying that he had married a California woman and wouldn't be returning. Her dress had been ready for two months. Her future husband even picked the pattern," she commented in disgust.

"Would it bother you to wear a dress that had been made for another who met with misfortune?" Mrs. O'Mallie asked.

"I don't think so," Delphinia answered. "It's so pretty and it's never been worn. Would they be willing to sell it, do you think?"

"It's mine." Miss Blodgett said. "Estelle was so devastated and Mary doesn't have the money to pay for a dress her daughter will never wear. I told them I'd take it apart and use the pieces for another gown. Would you like to try it on, Miss Hughes?"

"Oh, yes, I'd love to," she said, the excitement evident in her voice. "Unless you think it would make Estelle and her mother unhappy."

"I don't think they would mind a bit under the circumstances. Besides, your marriage won't even take place in Denver City," she responded.

"Then I'd like very much to see how it fits."

By the time they left the shop, Delphinia had purchased a properly fitted wedding dress, a matching veil, and a pair of shoes. Miss Blodgett was good to her word. She was able to stitch a few well-hidden tucks and the dress fit like it had been made for Delphinia. Mrs. O'Mallie was pleased because she had been able to convince Lucy to lower the price on the premise she was selling "previously purchased goods." That statement had caused a bit of a riff between the two older women, but eventually they came to terms. Delphinia, however, thought the dress was worth every cent of the original asking price.

The older women agreed that Delphinia made quite a spectacle in her finery, both feeling like they had championed a special cause.

Mrs. O'Mallie helped carry the purchases into the house and then bid Delphinia a quick farewell, knowing she would need to hurry with dinner preparations.

"Thank you again for all your assistance," Delphinia called after her as the older woman bustled out the back door.

Delphinia heard the jingle of her father's bedside bell and quickly hastened to his bedroom. "I thought I heard voices," he said, holding out his hand to beckon her forward. "Did you and Mrs. O'Mallie have success with your shopping?"

"Oh, Pa, we did! I purchased the most beautiful gown you could ever imagine. I know that God led me to it," she said smiling, as she proceeded to give him a detailed report of their shopping excursion.

"I'm looking forward to having you model it for me after dinner this evening," he said. "I wonder if Mrs. O'Mallie thinks she or God should have credit for leading you to that gown," he said with a small chuckle.

"I don't think she'd mind giving God some praise as long as she gets credit for Miss Blodgett's lowering the price," she answered, which caused them both to smile in appreciation of their neighbor's love of a bargain.

"I think I'll take a nap. I've been tired today," her father said, shifting in the bed to try and become more comfortable.

"How thoughtless of me. Here I've been rambling on while you need your rest. How's that?" she asked, adjusting his sheets.

"Fine, and you've not been rambling. It's given me more pleasure than you can imagine to hear you relate the events of today and I'm looking forward to seeing that dress on you a little later," he said, closing his eyes.

ও

Sam arrived home for dinner and although somewhat subdued, he remained cordial during their meal. The minute they finished, he rose from the table, informing Delphinia that he would be making house calls for the next several hours. As soon as he had departed, she ran next door to Mrs. O'Mallie's, requesting assistance buttoning her gown.

"I'll be over shortly," the older woman told her. "You get your hair fixed and by then I should be done in the kitchen."

Thirty minutes later, Mrs. O'Mallie came scurrying in the back doorway, proceeded to Delphinia's room, and her nimble fingers went to work closing the tiny pearl buttons that trailed down the back of the dress. "Now, let's put your veil on," she said after Delphinia had slipped her feet into the new white slippers. Carefully, Mrs. O'Mallie pulled curly tendrils of hair from behind the veil to frame either side of Delphinia's face.

"There! God never made a more beautiful bride," she said, stepping back and taking full view of the young woman. "Let's get you down the hall to your pa. You wait here in the hallway and I'll see if he's awake," Mrs. O'Mallie instructed.

Delphinia could hear Mrs. O'Mallie talking with her father, propping him up to permit a good view as she entered the room.

"All right. You can come in now," Mrs. O'Mallie called out.

Delphinia watched her father as she walked into the room. He appeared awe-struck after she pivoted in a full circle allowing him to see the entire dress. Turning back to face him, she watched a small tear slide down each of his sunken cheeks.

"I wish your mama could see you," he said, his voice cracking with emotion. "I know I've never seen such a pretty picture as you in that dress. Hasn't God been good to allow me such joy?"

"I'm glad you're pleased with my choice," Delphinia said, walking to the bed and placing a kiss on his damp cheek. "Thank you for accepting my decision to marry Jonathan, Papa, and thank you for this lovely wedding gift. I just wish you could be there for the wedding," she said.

"Your mama and I may not be with you in person, but we'll be there. You just remember that," he answered, trying to force his quivering lips into a smile.

"I know you will, I know," she answered.

"I think we better get this young lady out of her gown before she has it worn out," Mrs. O'Mallie said, trying to brighten the spirits of both father and daughter.

"We wouldn't want that," her father answered, "at least not until she's said her vows. You go ahead and change. We can visit again before you go to bed."

Delphinia returned once Mrs. O'Mallie had gone home. She sat by her father's bedside, visiting when he was awake and holding his hand as he slept, aware he was now in constant pain.

Later that night, a knock on her bedroom door awakened Delphinia from a sound sleep. Thinking she had overslept, her feet hit the floor before she realized it was still dark outside. Quickly, she pulled on her robe and rushed to open the door. Sam's eyes told it all.

"He's gone, isn't he?" she asked.

He nodded his head in affirmation. "I got home a few minutes ago and went in to check on him. He was dead. I'm sure he slipped away in his sleep," he said, watching her reaction, not sure how she would handle the news.

"He was ready," she said. "I know the pain had worn him down. What time is it?" she asked.

"Around five-thirty," he answered sheepishly. "I was gone longer than expected."

She did not respond to his comment, but knew from the odor of his breath that he had been drinking.

"I think I'll put on a pot of coffee. Mrs. O'Mallie will be up and about soon. She'll want to know. Why don't you get some sleep? There's nothing that needs to be done right now," she said, hoping he would take her suggestion.

"If you're all right, I'll do that. I have several calls to make later this morning and I'm going to need some rest," he responded.

"I'm fine. You go ahead," she answered, already lost in her own thoughts.

When Mrs. O'Mallie arrived, Delphinia was dressed and

sitting at the kitchen table, sipping her third cup of coffee.

"Aren't you the early bird? Coffee made and gone already," she said brightly.

Taking a closer look at the young woman, she saw her eyes were red and puffy. "Come here, child," she said, her arms outstretched to enfold and give comfort, her instincts telling her that death had come.

"Does Sam know?" Mrs. O'Mallie inquired.

"Yes, he went up to get some rest a little while ago. He didn't get much sleep last night," she answered without further explanation.

"I was hoping you would help me with the arrangements," Delphinia said, a sense of foreboding in her voice.

"Of course, I will. In fact, I'll take care of as much or as little as you'd like. You just tell me how much help you want," Mrs. O'Mallie answered, patting the younger woman's hand.

"Perhaps if you would go with me?" Delphinia asked. "Oh, and, Mrs. O'Mallie, I was wondering. . ." She paused, not sure how to proceed.

"Yes? Come now, Delphinia, you can ask me anything," the older woman urged.

"I don't think it would be proper for me to remain in Dr. Finley's house. Would you mind very much if I stayed with you until after the funeral? I'll leave just as soon as I can make travel arrangements," she said apologetically.

"I would love to have you come stay with me. If I would have been thinking straight I would have already offered. Why don't you pack your things while I get myself ready," she replied, already heading for the door.

Two days later, Mrs. O'Mallie and Sam Finley took Delphinia to meet the stage heading east out of Denver City.

eighteen

The journey by stage was tiring but the air was cool and Delphinia felt exhilarated to be on her way home. The stage was on schedule, allowing her to make the train connections and the trip home, although long, went smoothly. Her body ached for rest, however, and she wished she had been able to notify Jonathan of her arrival.

The train lurched to a stop and the conductor walked the aisle of the coach calling out, "Council Grove." Wearily, Delphinia made her way to the end of the coach where the conductor assisted her to the platform. "We'll have your trunk unloaded in just a few minutes, ma'am. You can wait in the station," he said politely.

She nodded and thanked him, too tired to be concerned about her trunk. The station was empty of customers and Delphinia sat on one of the two long wooden benches, waiting as instructed.

Her eyes fluttered open when she heard a voice asking, "Do you often sleep in train stations, Phiney?"

Looking down at her were those two beautiful blue eyes that belonged to the man she loved. "Jonathan, how did you. . .? Why are you. . .? What. . .?" she stammered.

"I don't believe you're quite awake. Seems like you can't get your words out," he said with a smile, lifting her into his arms and lightly kissing her lips.

"I don't. . . We ought not. . ."

"Seems my kiss wasn't quite enough to waken you. You're still stammering. I must be out of practice," he said and once again covered her mouth, enjoying the sweetness of her.

"Oh, Jonathan, I've missed you so. It's even good to be called Phiney," she said when he finally released her. "It seems I've been gone forever and so much has happened. How did you know I would be here?"

"I didn't know for sure, but I got a letter from your pa yesterday saying if things went as planned, he expected you'd be back today. I decided I wasn't going to miss the opportunity to meet your train. I checked the schedules and knew you couldn't make connections for another three days if you didn't get here today," he answered.

"You got a letter from Pa? Isn't that amazing," she said, wonderment on her face.

"Well, Mrs. O'Mallie had written it for him."

"Oh, I realize he didn't write it," she said. "I'm amazed because he wrote a letter telling you when I'd be home before he took a turn for the worse and died. It's almost as if he planned just what he wanted to accomplish and then died," she responded.

"I didn't know. . . I'm so sorry," he began.

"I know. It's all right," she answered. "Papa was ready to meet the Lord and I know he and Mama are enjoying their reunion," she said with a smile.

"Where are the children?" she asked, finally looking around to see if they were outside the station.

"Guess I was selfish. I left them at home with Maggie," he answered

"Maggie?" she questioned.

"Maggie Landry, the widow who's been helping while you were gone," he responded.

"I guess I left in such a rush, I never knew her name. I only remembered that Jennie O'Laughlin knew of a widow. How has she worked out? Do the children like her? Is she a good cook? You and Tessie never mentioned her when you wrote and I guess I didn't think to ask," she said, her voice suddenly full of concern.

"I didn't worry too much about her cooking and cleaning or whether the children liked her," he answered, his voice serious. "She's such a beauty, I didn't care about her home-making abilities," he said and then seeing the look on her face, broke into gales of laughter.

"She's probably close to sixty years old, Phiney!" His laughter continued until Delphinia stomped her foot in agitation and insisted he quiet down.

"Jonathan Wilshire, I was merely inquiring about the woman's expertise. You make it sound as though I were jealous," she said with an air of indignation.

"Weren't you? Now don't answer too quickly, Phiney. I don't want you to have to ask forgiveness for telling a lie," he said with a grin.

He watched her face as she tried to think of just the right answer. "Perhaps, just a little, but then my jealousy was quickly replaced by pity for the poor woman, since she'd have to put up with you and your antics if you took a fancy to her," she answered smugly.

"Is that so?" he asked, once again kissing her soundly as he lifted her onto the seat of the wagon. "You stay put until I get your trunk loaded. If I don't get you home soon, I know five little Wilshires that are going to have my hide."

"I'm not planning on going anywhere without you again," she said, smiling down at him.

≈

The reunion with the children was full of chaos. The twins greeted her with sounds of "Mama" and clung to her skirt while the boys tried to shout over each other to be heard. In the midst of the confusion, Tessie and Mrs. Landry tried to get dinner on the table.

The meal reminded Delphinia of the day she and Jonathan had first come to Kansas. It seemed like yesterday and yet, in other ways, it was a lifetime ago. This was her home now. This was where she belonged.

After dinner, Jonathan hitched the horses to the buggy and delivered Mrs. Landry back home for a much-needed rest, leaving Tessie and Delphinia to visit while cleaning the kitchen. They had talked of the children's antics while she had been gone and news of neighbors, school, and church, when Delphinia mentioned her surprise at finding the quilt top in her trunk.

"I was pleased you sent your quilt top with me," Delphinia said. "I didn't find it until I had been in Denver City for over a week. I didn't unpack my trunk right away, thinking I'd be able to return sooner," she confided.

"I was afraid you wouldn't come back to us. I'm sure Denver City is wonderful and full of excitement. I guess I thought if I sent the quilt along, you'd be sure and return," Tessie said sheepishly.

"It was more special for me to find that quilt top than almost anything you can imagine, Tessie, and we're going to begin work on it right away," she said just as Jonathan came into the room.

"I don't think so," he said, interrupting their conversation.

"Why not?" they asked in unison.

"Because I plan on keeping you occupied for the next week or so," he said sternly.

"Is that so?" she responded, rising to the challenge in his voice.

"I've sure missed being able to spar with you, gal," he said with a laugh. "But the fact is, I intend to have a wedding right away and spend a few days with you all to myself. What have you got to say to that?" he asked.

"I'd say it sounds wonderful," she answered. "I'm sure Tessie would allow us a little time before we start our project.

Especially if she knows I've found something special for the binding on her quilt," she remarked, watching Tessie's eyes light up with anticipation.

"What did you get? Please show me and then I promise I'll be off to bed," she begged.

"I think she's convinced me," said Jonathan.

Delphinia opened the trunk that Jonathan had placed just inside the door and, reaching down along one side with her hand, she pulled out a roll of soft fabric. With a smile that showed her pleasure, she placed the coil of lustrous ivory fabric in Tessie's hands.

"Oh, it's so elegant. Where did you ever find it?" Tessie asked.

"It's the same material that my wedding dress is made from. When I was being fitted for my gown, I told the shopkeeper about the quilt we were going to finish when I returned to Kansas. She suggested we might like to use the leftover fabric from my gown. I hoped you would like the idea," she answered.

"How could I not like it?" she asked, giving Delphinia a hug.

"And now, young lady, off to bed," Jonathan said. "I'd like to visit with Phiney a little while before I go over to my cabin. It's not too cool outside. Why don't we sit on the porch?" Jonathan said, moving toward the door.

Once they were seated, he continued, "I know you're tired and I don't plan to keep you up long, but I hope you'll consent to our being married a week from Saturday. Mrs. Aplington and the other women at church have already begun planning the festivities for afterward, and I announced in church we'd be getting married on your return. The preacher says he'll keep the date open and I've got some ideas about a wedding trip. You've got your wedding dress, so there's nothing to hold us back," he said convincingly.

"I think that sounds fine, except I don't want to go on a wedding trip. I've just gotten home," she answered.

"Don't you think we need a little time alone, without the children around?" he asked, not wanting to sound selfish but sure he did not want to marry and return home to the five children on their wedding day.

"What would you think about our staying at your cabin for a week or so after we're married? Just the two of us. We could see if Maggie would stay with the children, but we'd still be close by."

"I think that would be just fine," he answered, giving her a hug. "It's so good to have you home. You can't imagine how must I've missed you. Now I think I'd better let you get some rest. I'll see you in the morning," he said and gave her a kiss.

She stood on the porch watching as he made his way toward the smaller cabin. He was almost to his cabin when he turned and shouted loudly, "I love you, Phiney."

Smiling, she turned and walked into the house, savoring the pure joy of being back home with her Kansas family.

๛

A light tap on the door awakened Delphinia from a sound sleep and she was surprised to see the sun already beginning its ascent. A cool autumn breeze drifted through the small bedroom window as she called out, "Who is it?"

"Just me," came Tessie's voice. "May I come in?" she asked.

"Of course, you can," Delphinia answered and watched as the young redhead walked into the room and plopped herself at the foot of the bed.

"How can you be sleeping like this? You're always first up and here it is your wedding day when you should be all fluttery or something, and you're sleeping like a baby," Tessie exclaimed, full of frustration that she was the only one awake on a day she considered should be full of excitement from dawn until dark.

"I'm not sure why I'm still asleep," Delphinia answered. "Perhaps because I wasn't able to doze off until a short time ago," she admitted.

"Well, now that you're awake, what do we do first?" Tessie questioned, beginning to bounce on the side of the bed, unable to control her anticipation.

"For starters, you can quit jostling the bed," Delphinia answered with a smile. "If you really want to help, you can get breakfast started. Jonathan will be through with chores before I get out of bed, at this rate," she said, throwing back the covers and swinging her feet over the side of the bed.

"Aw, that's not what I meant. I want to really do something. You know, for the wedding," Tessie replied.

"Wedding or not, we still have to eat breakfast, Tessie. The wedding isn't until this afternoon and we've got to finish our regular work before we can get ready," Delphinia prodded.

"Okay, I'll get breakfast started," she answered, somewhat disheartened.

Delphinia smiled inwardly at the girl's excitement over the wedding. *Seems like only yesterday, she didn't even want me on this homestead, and now you'd think this wedding was the greatest event of her life,* Delphinia mused, thankful that God had been so good to all of them.

By three o'clock, the appointed time to leave the cabin, Delphinia wasn't sure anything was ready. If Maggie Landry hadn't shown up early to help, they wouldn't have been to the church until dusk. Insistent that Jonathan not see her before the wedding, the Aplingtons agreed Delphinia would go to the church with them and Jonathan could bring the rest of the family in the buckboard. The twins protested vehemently when Delphinia began to leave,

Ned tugged on her gown, while Nettie kept calling after her in a tearful voice, trying to suck her thumb and cry at the same time.

Mrs. Aplington and some of the other women had been to the church earlier that day, carrying in food and bringing fall flowers from their gardens to decorate the church. Their handiwork was beautiful and Delphinia was touched by all they had done, but even more by their love and acceptance.

As she began her slow walk down the aisle to meet her future husband, Jonathan smiled broadly, noting she was pressing down the gathers in the skirt of her wedding dress as she walked to meet him. When she reached his side, Jonathan leaned down and whispered, "There's nothing to be nervous about, Phiney."

"I'm not nervous. I'm very calm," she replied, her quivering voice belying that statement.

"Now, Phiney, we're in the house of God and there you go, trying to fib to me," he muttered back.

"Why are you trying to upset me, Jonathan?" she questioned, her voice louder than she intended, causing the guests to wonder just what was taking place.

The pastor loudly cleared his throat and whispered to both of them, "May we begin?"

"Well, I wish you would. We're in our places," came Delphinia's feisty response.

"She's something, isn't she?" Jonathan remarked to the preacher with a broad smile. "Sorry for the delay, but I wanted her to relax and enjoy the wedding. She needs to get a little fired up before she can calm down," he said to the pastor who merely shook his head, not sure he even wanted to try and understand that explanation.

As they exchanged their vows and pledged their love, Delphinia knew her parents and Granny were with them. In fact, if the truth were known, Granny was probably up in heaven impatiently tapping her foot and saying, "It's about time!"

The festivities were still in full swing at the church when the young couple made their way back to his house.

"Tessie said she put something in the back of the buggy for us," Delphinia advised Jonathan when they arrived at his cabin.

Reaching behind him, he pulled out a wicker basket. The handle was wrapped with white ribbon and topped with two large bows. Entering the house, he placed it on a small wooden table and then returned to the buggy, lifted Delphinia into his arms, and carried her into the cabin.

Placing her on the floor in front of him, he gathered her into his arms and kissed her with such passion, she felt her body go limp as she leaned against him. "That, Mrs. Wilshire, is how I intend to be kissed every morning, noon, and evening from now on," he announced, being careful to hold her upright.

"I'm not sure how much work I'll get done if you kiss me like that all day long," she answered with a smile.

"Let's see what Tessie sent along for us," he said, keeping her by his side as he lifted the covering from the basket.

"Looks like she didn't want you to spend your first day of married life having to cook for me," he told her. She peeked around him and saw fried chicken, a jar of homemade preserves, two loaves of bread, pickles, and sandwiches that had been cut into heart shapes, causing both of them to smile.

"There's a note in here, too. I'll let you open it," he said.

The note was written on a heart-shaped piece of paper and on the outside it said, *Before you open this, walk into the bedroom.*

Jonathan took her hand, guiding her into the small bedroom, and watched as Delphinia's face shone with absolute joy. "Oh, Jonathan, it's my quilt. How did you ever get my quilt back?"

"I didn't," he said. "The last time we were in town Tessie saw the Indian who had been to the cabin. He was carrying your quilt over his arm. There was no holding her back. She went straight to him and the next thing I knew, she had his knife and was cutting off some more of her hair. I sat watching to make sure nothing would happen. A short time later she returned to the wagon with your quilt," he answered.

"What does her note say?" he asked.

She opened it and read out loud,

> *Dearest Delphinia and Jonathan,*
> *May the threads of love that hold this quilt, tie your hearts with love and joy forever.*
>
> *Love,*
> *Tessie.*

A Letter To Our Readers

Dear Reader:

In order that we might better contribute to your reading enjoyment, we would appreciate your taking a few minutes to respond to the following questions. When completed, please return to the following:

Rebecca Germany, Managing Editor
Heartsong Presents
P.O. Box 719
Uhrichsville, Ohio 44683

1. Did you enjoy reading *Threads of Love?*
   ❑ Very much. I would like to see more books
      by this author!
   ❑ Moderately
      I would have enjoyed it more if _____

   _____

2. Are you a member of **Heartsong Presents**? ❑Yes ❑No
   If no, where did you purchase this book?_____

   _____

3. What influenced your decision to purchase this
   book? (Check those that apply.)

   ❑ Cover   ❑ Back cover copy

   ❑ Title   ❑ Friends

   ❑ Publicity   ❑ Other_____

4. How would you rate, on a scale from 1 (poor) to 5
   (superior), the cover design?_____

5. On a scale from 1 (poor) to 10 (superior), please rate the following elements.

    ___Heroine   ___Plot

    ___Hero   ___Inspirational theme

    ___Setting   ___Secondary characters

6. What settings would you like to see covered in **Heartsong Presents** books?_____

_____

_____

7. What are some inspirational themes you would like to see treated in future books?_____

_____

_____

8. Would you be interested in reading other **Heartsong Presents** titles?   ❏ Yes   ❏ No

9. Please check your age range:
    ❏ Under 18   ❏ 18-24   ❏ 25-34
    ❏ 35-45   ❏ 46-55   ❏ Over 55

10. How many hours per week do you read? _____

Name _____

Occupation _____

Address _____

City_____ State_____ Zip _____

Summer Dreams

*Four all-new inspirational novellas
with all the romance of a summer's day.*

Summer Breezes **by Veda Boyd Jones**
Law school graduate Melina Howard takes on Blake Allen, a
former sailing instructor, as her crew in a local regatta.

A la Mode **by Yvonne Lehman**
Small town florist Heather Willis is intrigued when she makes
the acquaintance of a mysterious stranger with a Texan accent.

King of Hearts **by Tracie J. Peterson**
Elise Jost is a non-traditional student whose life's direction
takes a different course when she makes a high grade with
professor Ian Hunter.

No Groom for the Wedding **by Kathleen Yapp**
A professional photographer, Penny Blake is capturing her
sister's honeymoon when she finds herself the focus of a fellow
cruise passenger.

(352 pages, Paperbound, 5" x 8")

·····Hearts♥ng·····

HEARTSONG PRESENTS TITLES AVAILABLE NOW:

(If ordering from this page, please remember to include it with the order form.)

········ Presents ········

Great Inspirational Romance at a Great Price!

Heartsong Presents books are inspirational romances in contemporary and historical settings, designed to give you an enjoyable, spirit-lifting reading experience. You can choose wonderfully written titles from some of today's best authors like Peggy Darty, Tracie J. Peterson, Colleen L. Reece, Lauraine Snelling, and many others.

When ordering quantities less than twelve, above titles are $2.95 each.

Heart❤ng Presents
Love Stories Are Rated G!

That's for godly, gratifying, and of course, great! If you love a thrilling love story, but don't appreciate the sordidness of some popular paperback romances, **Heartsong Presents** is for you. In fact, **Heartsong Presents** is the *only inspirational romance book club*, the only one featuring love stories where Christian faith is the primary ingredient in a marriage relationship.

Sign up today to receive your first set of four, never before published Christian romances. Send no money now; you will receive a bill with the first shipment. You may cancel at any time without obligation, and if you aren't completely satisfied with any selection, you may return the books for an immediate refund!

Imagine...four new romances every four weeks—two historical, two contemporary—with men and women like you who long to meet the one God has chosen as the love of their lives...all for the low price of $9.97 postpaid.

To join, simply complete the coupon below and mail to the address provided. **Heartsong Presents** romances are rated G for another reason: They'll arrive *Godspeed!*